Much Ado About Nothing

無事生非

商務印書館

This Chinese edition of *Much Ado About Nothing* has been published with the written permission of Black Cat Publishing.

The copyright of this Chinese edition is owned by The Commercial Press (H.K.) Ltd.

Name of Book: Much Ado About Nothing
Author: William Shakespeare
Text adaptation: James Butler
Notes and activities: Kenneth Brodey
Editors: Rebecca Raynes, Alex Smith
Design: Nadia Maestri
Illustrations: Giovanni Manna
Edition: ©2001 Black Cat Publishing
    an imprint of Cideb Editrice, Genoa, Canterbury

系 列 名：Black Cat 優質英語階梯閱讀 · Level 5
書　　名：無事生非
責任編輯：傅　伊
封面設計：張　毅　曹　磊
出　　版：商務印書館（香港）有限公司
　　　　　香港筲箕灣耀興道 3 號東滙廣場 8 樓
　　　　　http://www.commercialpress.com.hk
發　　行：香港聯合書刊物流有限公司
　　　　　香港新界大埔汀麗路 36 號中華商務印刷大廈 3 字樓
印　　刷：中華商務彩色印刷有限公司
　　　　　香港新界大埔汀麗路 36 號中華商務印刷大廈
版　　次：2013 年 5 月第 1 版第 2 次印刷
　　　　　© 商務印書館（香港）有限公司
　　　　　ISBN 978 962 07 1665 2
　　　　　Printed in Hong Kong

版權所有　不得翻印

出版説明

　　本館一向倡導優質閱讀，近年來連續推出了以 "Q" 為標識的 "Quality English Learning 優質英語學習" 系列，其中《讀名著學英語》叢書，更是香港書展入選好書，讀者反響令人鼓舞。推動社會閱讀風氣，推動英語經典閱讀，藉閱讀拓廣世界視野，提高英語水平，已經成為一種潮流。

　　然良好閱讀習慣的養成非一日之功，大多數初、中級程度的讀者，常視直接閱讀厚重的原著為畏途。如何給年輕的讀者提供切實的指引和幫助，如何既提供優質的學習素材，又提供名師的教學方法，是當下社會關注的重要問題。針對這種情況，本館特別延請香港名校名師，根據多年豐富的教學經驗，精選海外適合初、中級英語程度讀者的優質經典讀物，有系統地出版了這套叢書，名為《Black Cat 優質英語階梯閱讀》。

　　《Black Cat 優質英語階梯閱讀》體現了香港名校名師堅持經典學習的教學理念，以及多年行之有效的學習方法。既有經過改寫和縮寫的經典名著，又有富創意的現代作品；既有精心設計的聽、説、讀、寫綜合練習，又有豐富的歷史文化知識；既有彩色插圖、繪圖和照片，又有英美專業演員朗讀作品的 CD。適合口味不同的讀者享受閱讀之樂，欣賞經典之美。

　　《Black Cat 優質英語階梯閱讀》由淺入深，逐階提升，好像參與一個尋寶遊戲，入門並不難，但要真正尋得寶藏，需要投入，更需要堅持。只有置身其中的人，才能體味純正英語的魅力，領略得到真寶的快樂。當英語閱讀成為自己生活的一部分，英語水平的提高自然水到渠成。

商務印書館（香港）有限公司
編輯部

使用説明

 應該怎樣選書？

按閱讀興趣選書

《Black Cat 優質英語階梯閱讀》精選世界經典作品，也包括富於創意的現代作品；既有膾炙人口的小說、戲劇，又有非小說類的文化知識讀物，品種豐富，內容多樣，適合口味不同的讀者挑選自己感興趣的書，享受閱讀的樂趣。

按英語程度選書

《Black Cat 優質英語階梯閱讀》現設 Level 1 至 Level 6，由淺入深，涵蓋初、中級英語程度。讀物分級採用了國際上通用的劃分標準，主要以詞彙（vocabulary）和結構（structures）劃分。

Level 1 至 Level 3 出現的詞彙較淺顯，相對深的核心詞彙均配上中文解釋，節省讀者查找詞典的時間，以專心理解正文內容。在註釋的幫助下，讀者若能流暢地閱讀正文內容，就不用擔心這一本書程度過深。

Level 1 至 Level 3 出現的動詞時態形式和句子結構比較簡單。動詞時態形式以現在時（present simple）、現在時進行式（present continuous）、過去時（past simple）為主，句子結構大部分是簡單句（simple sentences）。此外，還包括比較級和最高級（comparative and superlative forms）、可數和不可數名詞（countable and uncountable nouns）以及冠詞（articles）等語法知識點。

Level 4 至 Level 6 出現的動詞時態形式，以現在完成時（present perfect）、現在完成時進行式（present perfect continuous）、過去完成時（past perfect continuous）為主，句子結構大部分是複合句（compound sentences）、條件從句（1st and 2nd conditional sentences）等。此外，還包括情態動詞（modal verbs）、被動形式（passive forms）、動名詞（gerunds）、

短語動詞（phrasal verbs）等語法知識點。

根據上述的語法範圍，讀者可按自己實際的英語水平，如詞彙量、語法知識、理解能力、閱讀能力等自主選擇，不再受制於學校年級劃分或學歷高低的約束，完全根據個人需要選擇合適的讀物。

◆ ② 怎樣提高閱讀效果？

閱讀的方法主要有兩種：一是泛讀，二是精讀。兩者各有功能，適當地結合使用，相輔相成，有事半功倍之效。

泛讀，指閱讀大量適合自己程度（可稍淺，但不能過深）、不同內容、風格、體裁的讀物，但求明白內容大意，不用花費太多時間鑽研細節，主要作用是多接觸英語，減輕對它的生疏感，鞏固以前所學過的英語，讓腦子在潛意識中吸收詞彙用法、語法結構等。

精讀，指小心認真地閱讀內容精彩、組織有條理、遣詞造句又正確的作品，着重點在於理解 "準確" 及 "深入"，欣賞其精彩獨到之處。精讀時，可充分利用書中精心設計的練習，學習掌握有用的英語詞彙和語法知識。精讀後，可再花十分鐘朗讀其中一小段有趣的文字，邊唸邊細心領會文字的結構和意思。

《Black Cat 優質英語階梯閱讀》中的作品均值得精讀，如時間有限，不妨嘗試每兩個星期泛讀一本，輔以每星期挑選書中一章精彩的文字精讀。要學好英語，持之以恆地泛讀和精讀英文是最有效的方法。

◆ ③ 本系列的練習與測試有何功能？

《Black Cat 優質英語階梯閱讀》特別注重練習的設計，為讀者考慮周到，切合實用需求，學習功能強。每章後均配有訓練聽、說、讀、寫四項技能的練習，分量、難度恰到好處。

聽力練習分兩類，一是重聽故事回答問題，二是聆聽主角對話、書信朗讀、或模擬記者訪問後寫出答案，旨在以生活化的練習形式逐步提高聽力。每本書均配有 CD 提供作品朗讀，朗讀者都是專業演員，英國作品由英國演員錄音，美國作品由美國演員錄音，務求增加聆聽的真實感和感染力。多聆聽英式和美式英語兩種發音，可讓讀者熟悉二者的差異，逐漸培養分辨英美發音的能力，提高聆聽理解的準確度。此外，模仿錄音朗讀故事或模仿主人翁在戲劇中的對白，都是訓練口語能力的好方法。

閱讀理解練習形式多樣化，有縱橫字謎、配對、填空、字句重組等等，注重訓練讀者的理解、推敲和聯想等多種閱讀技能。

寫作練習尤具新意，教讀者使用網式圖示（spidergrams）記錄重點，採用問答、書信、電報、記者採訪等多樣化形式，鼓勵讀者動手寫作。

書後更設有升級測試（Exit Test）及答案，供讀者檢查學習效果。充分利用書中的練習和測試，可全面提升聽、說、讀、寫四項技能。

◆ 4 本系列還能提供甚麼幫助？

《Black Cat 優質英語階梯閱讀》提倡豐富多元的現代閱讀，巧用書中提供的資訊，有助於提升英語理解力，擴闊視野。

每本書都設有專章介紹相關的歷史文化知識，經典名著更有作者生平、社會背景等資訊。書內富有表現力的彩色插圖、繪圖和照片，使閱讀充滿趣味，部分加上如何解讀古典名畫的指導，增長見識。有的書還提供一些與主題相關的網址，比如關於不同國家的節慶源流的網址，讓讀者多利用網上資源增進知識。

Contents

FCE : First Certificate in English Examination-style exercises.

This story is recorded in full. 故事錄音

 END These symbols indicate the beginning and end of
the extracts linked to the listening activities.
聽力練習開始和結束的標記

SHAKESPEARE'S LIFE

W illiam Shakespeare was born in Stratford-upon-Avon in 1564. It is thought that he was born on 23 April. William Shakespeare's father was John Shakespeare, a merchant who played an important role in the politics of Stratford-upon-Avon. John Shakespeare married Mary Arden, and they had 8 children. He became bailiff [1] and justice of the peace [2] in 1568. In later years the business fortunes of John Shakespeare declined.[3] It is not known where the young William Shakespeare went to school, although it is thought that he attended the local grammar school, where pupils were instructed in Latin.

Shakespeare married Anne Hathaway when he was 18 years old, and the couple had 3 children – a daughter, Susanna, who was born in 1583, and twins, Hamnet and Judith, who were born in 1585.

How Shakespeare earned his living as a young adult is not known, although there is some evidence that he may have been a schoolmaster. It is not known, either, how he first entered the world of the theatre. According to one story, an actor in the Queen's Company died shortly before the company visited Stratford-upon-Avon in 1587; it is said that Shakespeare took the dead man's place.

The first reference to Shakespeare is in a pamphlet written in 1592. The pamphlet

1. **bailiff** : an officer whose job is to make sure that a court order is carried out.
2. **justice of the peace** : a person who judges less serious cases in a lawcourt in Britain.
3. **declined** : became less good.

shows that Shakespeare was already established [1] in the theatrical world by that date. By 1594 Shakespeare was an important member of the Lord Chamberlain's Men, a theatrical company based in London. The company played at the Globe Theatre from 1599 onwards, and changed their name to the King's Men in 1603. In 1608 the King's Men moved to the Blackfriar's Theatre.

Shakespeare wrote 38 plays for the theatre before he died in 1616, as well as poetry and the most famous series of sonnets in the English language. His work was gathered together and published after his death. Visitors to Stratford-upon-Avon can visit many places associated with the playwright's life, including the house where he was born and Anne Hathaway's cottage. They can also visit the Royal Shakespeare Theatre and see performances of his plays.

1 Answer the following questions. Indicate which answers are CERTAIN and which ones are just LIKELY.

a. Where was Shakespeare born?
He was born in Stratford-on-Avon. .... CERTAIN ....

b. When was he born?
....

c. Who were his parents?
....

d. Where did he go to school?
....

e. How old was Shakespeare when he got married?
....

f. How many children did he have and what were their names?
....

g. What jobs did Shakespeare do before becoming an actor?
....

h. How did Shakespeare get his first acting job?
....

i. Which theatrical companies did he work with?
....

j. When were his theatrical works published?
....

1. **established** : having a permanent position.

SHAKESPEARE'S
Much Ado About Nothing

M uch Ado About Nothing was probably written between 1598 and 1599. It is a comedy about love. The action of the play begins with the visit of the Prince of Aragon, Don Pedro, to Messina, where he is the guest of Leonato. One of Don Pedro's officers, Claudio, falls in love with Leonato's daughter, Hero. Don Pedro helps Claudio to win Leonato's permission for the marriage. The Prince's brother, Don John, is determined to destroy the relationship between Claudio and Hero. He enters into a plot with his friend Borachio to make it seem that Hero already has a lover.

Claudio's best friend is another young officer called Benedick. Benedick is well-known for his humour, and his determination never to fall in love. The Prince and Claudio decide to play a trick on him by making him believe that Leonato's niece, Beatrice, is in love with him. They also try to persuade Beatrice that Benedick is in love with her.

Claudio is very angry when he discovers that Hero seems to have a lover, and he decides to humiliate [1] her at the wedding ceremony. He denounces [2] her in

Scene from Much Ado About Nothing *(1789)*
by Johann Heinrich Füssli.
Gemäldegalerie Alte Meister, Dresden.

1. **humiliate** : make somebody feel ashamed.
2. **denounces** : says publicly that something is wrong.

11

front of the guests, and refuses to marry her. Hero faints with shock in the church, and Claudio and Don Pedro believe that she is dead.

The local constables, Dogberry and Verges, soon discover Don John's plot against Claudio and the Prince. Claudio is full of remorse [1] when he learns the truth. Leonato tells Claudio that he was responsible for Hero's death, and asks him to marry one of Hero's cousins. Claudio agrees to do this, in order to make amends [2] for his cruelty to Hero. When Claudio arrives at the wedding he is amazed to discover that the 'cousin' is really Hero herself. Benedick interrupts the proceedings [3] to ask if he can marry Beatrice. The play ends happily with all the problems resolved.

Who's who

1 **Answer the following questions.**

   a. Who visits Leonato?

   ....

   b. Who are the two officers of this visitor?

   ....

   c. Who is Leonato's daughter?

   ....

   d. Who is Leonato's niece?

   ....

   e. Who falls in love with Hero?

   ....

   f. Who plays a trick on Benedick?

   ....

   g. Who never wants to fall in love?

   ....

   h. Who faints in the church?

   ....

   i. Who plots against the lovers?

   ....

   j. Who discover the plot?

   ....

1. **remorse** : a feeling of sadness because you have done something wrong.
2. **make amends** : compensate.
3. **proceedings** : events that happen at a formal ceremony.

Before you read

1 Fill in the gaps in the text with suitable words. Then listen and check.

Leonato, the Governor of Messina, 0.........was.......... walking in the city with his daughter Hero and his niece Beatrice. The two young women were 1......................... beautiful, and they chatted happily to 2......................... other as they went along. Leonato watched them both with a smile. He, too, was contented.

Suddenly a messenger appeared 3......................... the far end of the street. He was looking 4......................... the Governor. 5......................... he saw Leonato, he ran up to him with a letter in 6......................... hand. He bowed in front of the Governor, and handed him 7......................... letter.

Leonato opened the letter and read 8......................... quickly.

'Is Don Pedro coming here?' he 9......................... the messenger.

'Yes, sir,' the messenger replied. 'The Prince of Aragon 10......................... coming to Messina. He 11......................... arrive shortly.'

'He says here that the army had a great victory,' Leonato said. 'Did we lose 12......................... soldiers in the battle?'

'No, sir,' the messenger said proudly. 'Very 13......................... of our men were 14........................., I am happy to say.'

Leonato was pleased.

'That's good news,' he commented. He turned to the letter again. 'I see that Don Pedro 15......................... very pleased with the young Florentine, Claudio.'

'True, sir,' the messenger confirmed. 'The Prince 16......................... honoured Claudio for his courage in the battle.

'What 17......................... Benedick?' Beatrice asked the messenger. 'Have you got any news about him?'

'He, too, has come home safely,' the messenger replied politely. 'He is famous for his humour.'

'I'm glad 18 .... hear that he's famous for his humour,' Beatrice said coldly. 'It's the only good thing about him.'

The messenger looked at Beatrice in surprise. He thought she was being rude about Benedick, and he 19......................... not know 20......................... to reply to her.

Dramatis Personae

DON PEDRO
Prince of Aragon

DON JOHN
his brother

CLAUDIO
a young Lord of Florence

LEONATO
Governor of Messina

ANTONIO
his brother

BENEDICK
a young Lord of Padua

BORACHIO and CONRAD
followers of Don John

BEATRICE
Niece to Leonato

HERO
Daughter to Leonato

MARGARET and URSULA
waiting-gentlewomen of Hero

FRIAR FRANCIS

BALTHAZAR
servant to Don Pedro

DOGBERRY
a Constable

VERGES
a Headborough

CHAPTER ONE

Love at First Sight

Leonato, the Governor of Messina, was walking in the city with his daughter Hero and his niece Beatrice. The two young women were both beautiful, and they chatted happily to each other as they went along. Leonato watched them both with a smile. He, too, was contented.

Suddenly, a messenger appeared at the far end of the street. He was looking for the Governor. When he saw Leonato, he ran up to him with a letter in his hand. He bowed [1] in front of the Governor, and handed him the letter.

1. **bowed** :

Much Ado About Nothing

Leonato opened the letter and read it quickly.

'Is Don Pedro coming here?' he asked the messenger.

'Yes, sir,' the messenger replied. 'The Prince of Aragon is coming to Messina. He will arrive soon.'

'He says here that the army had a great victory,' Leonato said. 'Did we lose many soldiers [1] in the battle?'

'No, sir,' the messenger said proudly. 'Very few of our men were killed, I am happy to say.'

Leonato was pleased.

'That's good news,' he commented. He turned to the letter again. 'I see that Don Pedro is very pleased with the young Florentine, Claudio.'

'True, sir,' the messenger confirmed. 'The Prince has honoured Claudio for his courage in the battle.'

'What about Benedick?' Beatrice asked the messenger. 'Have you got any news about him?'

'He, too, has come home safely,' the messenger replied politely. 'He is famous for his humour.'

'I'm glad to hear that he's famous for his humour,' Beatrice said coldly. 'It's the only good thing about him.'

The messenger looked at Beatrice in surprise. He thought she was being rude about Benedick, and he did not know how to reply to her.

Leonato saw that the messenger was embarrassed.

'It's all right,' he told the man with a laugh. 'Don't think my niece is serious. Beatrice and Benedick are always telling jokes about each other – she doesn't mean any harm.'

'But tell me,' Beatrice said to the messenger, 'has Benedick got a new friend in the army? He seems to change his best friend every month.'

'Is that really true?' the messenger asked.

---

1. **Did we lose many soldiers** : were many soldiers killed?

Love at First Sight

'Of course it is,' Beatrice said firmly. 'A friendship is like a hat to Benedick – it lasts until there is a new fashion!'

'I see that Benedick is not in your good books,'[1] the messenger said.

'That's true,' Beatrice replied quickly. 'If Benedick were in my good books, I would never read them again. But you haven't told me – who is Benedick's new friend?'

'Benedick and Claudio are good friends,' the messenger told her. 'They are both brave young men.'

At that moment the Prince of Aragon, Don Pedro, came into the street. There was a crowd of people with him. The messenger could see the Prince's brother, Don John, and several young soldiers, including Benedick and Claudio.

Leonato stepped forward to greet the Prince.

'Welcome to Messina,' he said politely. 'I am happy that you will be my guest while you are here.'

Don Pedro shook Leonato's hand. Then he looked at Hero.

'Is this your daughter?' he asked.

'Yes, indeed,' Leonato replied. Then he made a little joke. 'At least her mother has always said Hero is my daughter!'

'Her mother tells you!' Benedick interrupted. 'Do you doubt it, sir?' he joked.

Leonato smiled at the young man. He was not offended,[2] because he knew Benedick's reputation for jokes and humour.

'No sir,' he replied slowly, 'I do not doubt it. Why should I doubt it? You were still a child!'

Don Pedro laughed loudly.

'A good reply, my friend!' he said to Leonato. 'What do you say to that, Benedick?' he asked. 'The Governor means that you have a bad reputation with women!'

Everyone laughed at the Governor's joke except Beatrice. She looked angrily at Benedick.

1. **in your good books** : you have a high opinion of him.
2. **offended** : upset.

'What a fool you are,' she told him. 'Can't you see how everyone is laughing at you?'

Benedick did not like Beatrice. He turned to her with an ironical greeting.

'I see you're still alive, Lady Scornful,' [1] he said.

'Of course I'm still alive,' Beatrice replied mockingly. 'My scorn feeds off [2] you – didn't you know that?'

Benedick pretended to laugh at Beatrice's humour.

'All the ladies love me, except you,' he told her proudly. 'But I don't care for any of them.'

'Lucky women!' Beatrice said. 'At least you won't marry one of them and make her unhappy. But I'm like you,' she told him. 'I've got no patience with love.'

'Lucky men!' Benedick replied. 'At least you won't make one of them unhappy.'

Soon the large group of people began to move towards Leonato's house. There was a lot of laughing and joking. Everyone was happy. Claudio touched Benedick's arm, and held him back.

'Just a minute,' he said quietly. 'I want to talk to you.'

'What is it?' Benedick asked, when the two men were alone.

'Did you notice Leonato's daughter Hero?' Claudio asked his friend. 'Did you see how beautiful she is?'

'I didn't really notice her. She's not bad looking, but her cousin Beatrice is far more beautiful,' Benedick said thoughtfully.

'She's the most beautiful girl in the world!' Claudio announced firmly.

Benedick looked closely at his friend.

'You're in love!' he said slowly. 'But surely you're not thinking of getting married?'

Claudio frowned. [3]

'I've never thought about marriage before,' he admitted. 'But if Hero would marry me, I'd certainly be very happy!'

1. **scornful** : rude, critical of others.
2. **feeds off** : an insulting way of saying that someone uses something to continue their activities.
3. **frowned** : made an expression of disapproval or anger.

Love at First Sight

Benedick began to laugh.

'I don't understand you, my friend,' he said with a smile, 'but if it makes you happy, marry the girl!'

Just then Don Pedro returned to the young men.

'Why have you stayed behind?' he asked. 'What are you talking about? Is it a secret?'

Benedick began to laugh again. He told the Prince about Claudio's love for Hero.

'She's a fine girl,' the Prince told Claudio.

'You needn't laugh,' he told Benedick. 'You'll fall in love one day, as well!'

'Never!' Benedick told him. 'I like all women – I'll never surrender to just one woman.'[1]

Don Pedro smiled.

'You'll fall in love one day, my young friend,' he repeated. 'I shall see you pale with love one day.'

'Never!' Benedick said again. 'You may see me pale with illness, or pale with anger, my Lord – but you'll never see me pale with love. I promise you that!'

'We shall see, we shall see,' Don Pedro told him. 'Now go into the house with the others, Benedick – I want to have a serious talk with Claudio about all this.'

Benedick bowed politely to the Prince, and walked towards Leonato's house.

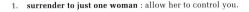

1. **surrender to just one woman** : allow her to control you.

Go back to the text

1 **Answer the following questions.**

    a. Who is the Governor of Messina?

    ....

    b. Who is he walking with in the city?

    ....

    c. What news does the messenger bring?

    ....

    d. Why isn't Leonato surprised at Beatrice's rudeness?

    ....

    e. Who is Claudio?

    ....

    f. Who is Benedick?

    ....

    g. What is Benedick famous for?

    ....

    h. How does Beatrice talk about Benedick?

    ....

    i. What does Beatrice mean when she says that for Benedick friendship is like a hat?

    ....

    j. Who does Claudio find beautiful?

    ....

'If Benedick were in my good books, I would never read them again.'

2 **Since this is a comedy, it is full of funny remarks. Find the ones in Chapter One which mean the following.**

    a. A man can never be really sure if his wife has been faithful, so he never knows if his children are really his.

    b. Every sort of terrible thing may happen to me, but never that terrible thing called love.

    c. I do not doubt my wife's faithfulness because you were only a child when she was a young woman.

    d. Men are lucky that you do not want to fall in love because any man would be terribly unhappy with you.

    e. My hate for you keeps me alive.

    f. He changes his friends all the time for no good reason.

'Beatrice and Benedick are always telling jokes about each other.'

> **Each other**
>
> To understand the use of the reciprocal pronoun *each other* look at the following example from Chapter One.
> *Beatrice and Benedick are always telling jokes about **each other**.* =
> Beatrice tells jokes about Benedick, and Benedick tells jokes about Beatrice.
>
> Reflexive pronouns (*myself, yourself, himself, herself, itself, ourselves, yourselves, themselves*) are used when the subject of the verb performs an action on him or herself.
>
> Look at the following example.
> *Beatrice and Benedick are always telling jokes about **themselves**.* =
> Beatrice tells jokes about Beatrice, and Benedick tells jokes about Benedick.

3 **Complete each gap with either a reciprocal pronoun or a reflexive pronoun to make a logical sentence.**

   a. Hero and Beatrice talk to .... as they walk down the streets of Messina.

   b. At the beginning of the play it seems that Beatrice and Benedick hate ....

   c. After they make their funny remarks Beatrice and Benedick are proud of ....

   d. When men and women are in love, they often spend a great deal of time looking at .... in the mirror before meeting their lovers.

   e. Men and women who are in love spend a great deal of time looking at ....

   f. Beatrice and Benedick cannot imagine .... being married.

   g. At the end of the play Beatrice and Benedick love ....

Before you read

1 **Listen to the first part of Chapter Two and indicate which of the synonyms (a, b or c) is actually used in the text.**

Don Pedro and Claudio watched Benedick walk away. Then they went into the garden of Leonato's house, and began to [1]........................ and down together.

'Well, my friend? What's all this about you and Hero?' the Prince asked gently.

'I think I love her,' Claudio told the Prince. 'I liked her when I saw her last, before we went away to the war. Now that I've seen her again, I'm 2......................... of it – that's the girl for me!'

'She's a good choice,' Don Pedro told him. 'She's a 3......................... girl, and she comes from a good family. But why are you so 4......................... Claudio?'

'Perhaps, she won't believe I love her!' Claudio said unhappily. 'Perhaps she'll think it's all too 5......................... .'

'6.........................,' Don Pedro said. '7......................... she'll believe you. And I'll do what I can to help you. Let me think for a minute.' The Prince and Claudio were silent, then the Prince laughed. 'I know what to do,' he said suddenly. 'There's going to be a big party at Leonato's house tonight. Everybody will be wearing masks. I'll talk to Hero. I'll pretend to be you, see?'

A servant was also in the garden that afternoon. He saw the two men walking together, and he was curious to know what they were talking about. The servant hid behind a tree to hear what was being said.

'Me?' Claudio repeated. 'I don't really 8......................... what you 9........................., sir.'

'10......................... it's 11.........................,' Don Pedro said impatiently. 'I'll go up to Hero, and I'll tell her I love her. I'll tell her I've always loved her, that I can't live without her. Then I'll go to her father and tell him everything.'

1.	**a.** promenade	**b.** walk slowly	**c.** stroll up
2.	**a.** certain	**b.** sure	**c.** positive
3.	**a.** lovely	**b.** beautiful	**c.** very attractive
4.	**a.** unhappy	**b.** sad	**c.** sorrowful
5.	**a.** quick	**b.** unexpected	**c.** sudden
6.	**a.** Ridiculous	**b.** Nonsense	**c.** Rubbish
7.	**a.** Of course	**b.** Certainly	**c.** Surely
8.	**a.** see	**b.** understand	**c.** get
9.	**a.** are trying to say	**b.** are driving at	**c.** mean
10.	**a.** Why	**b.** But	**c.** My goodness
11.	**a.** easy	**b.** simple	**c.** a piece of cake

CHAPTER TWO

A Strategy for Love

on Pedro and Claudio watched Benedick walk away. Then they went into the garden of Leonato's house, and began to stroll [1] up and down together.

'Well, my friend? What's all this about you and Hero?' the Prince asked gently.

'I think I love her,' Claudio told the Prince. 'I liked her when I saw her last, before we went away to the war. Now that I've seen her again, I'm sure of it – that's the girl for me!'

'She's a good choice,' Don Pedro told him. 'She's a beautiful girl, and she comes from a good family. But why are you so unhappy, Claudio?'

'Perhaps she won't believe I love her!' Claudio said unhappily. 'Perhaps she'll think it's all too sudden.'

---

1. **stroll** : walk slowly.

Much Ado About Nothing

'Nonsense,' Don Pedro said. 'Of course she'll believe you. And I'll do what I can to help you. Let me think for a minute.'

The Prince and Claudio were silent, then the Prince laughed. 'I know what to do,' he said suddenly. 'There's going to be a big party at Leonato's house tonight. Everybody will be wearing masks. [1] I'll talk to Hero. I'll pretend to be you, you see?'

A servant was also in the garden that afternoon. He saw the two men walking together, and he was curious to know what they were talking about. The servant hid behind a tree to hear what was being said.

'Me?' Claudio repeated. 'I don't really understand what you mean, sir.'

'Why, it's simple,' Don Pedro said impatiently. 'I'll go up to Hero, and I'll tell her I love her. I'll tell her I've always loved her, that I can't live without her. Then I'll go to her father and tell him everything.'

1.   masks :

26

A Strategy for Love

'Don Pedro's in love with Hero!' the servant said to himself. 'I must go and tell my master immediately!'

He ran quickly back into the house.

'Then you'll be able to marry her!' the Prince said triumphantly. 'What do you think of my plan, Claudio?'

Later that afternoon Leonato and his brother Antonio met in the great house. Antonio had been invited to the party, and he was in a very good mood. The two brothers greeted each other affectionately.

'I was looking for you,' Antonio said merrily. [1] 'I've got some extraordinary [2] news for you!'

'News? What kind of news?' Leonato asked.

'The Prince is in love with your daughter,' Antonio told him.

'Don Pedro in love with Hero?' Leonato said. He was very surprised. 'But how do you know this? Who told you?'

'One of my servants was in the garden earlier,' Antonio explained. 'He saw Don Pedro and Claudio talking together. He heard the Prince say that he would speak to Hero at the party tonight – he's going to tell her he loves her!'

'I can hardly believe it,' Leonato said thoughtfully. 'I'd better tell Hero about this – then she'll know what to do if the Prince speaks to her.'

Although most of Leonato's guests were looking forward to [3] the party, there was one man who refused to join in the general mood of rejoicing. [4] This was Don Pedro's illegitimate [5] brother, Don John. Don John was very

---

1. **merrily** : cheerfully.
2. **extraordinary** : very unusual.
3. **looking forward to** : waiting with pleasure for something to happen.
4. **rejoicing** : celebration.
5. **illegitimate** : born to parents who are not married to each other.

jealous of his brother, and he was always plotting [1] against him. One of his plots had recently failed, and the two brothers had only just become friends again.

One of Don John's friends was Conrad.

'You should be more cheerful, sir,' Conrad advised. 'You and the Prince are friends again. Everything is going well.'

'I can't help it,' Don John told him. 'I don't feel cheerful. I don't like my brother, and I'm forced to be polite to him.'

Just then another of Don John's friends came into the room.

'What's the news, Borachio?' Don John asked.

Borachio smiled.

'There is news, sir,' he announced. 'Claudio is going to marry Hero.'

'How do you know?' Don John asked quickly.

'I heard Don Pedro and Claudio talking in the house,' Borachio told him. 'They've made a plan. Don Pedro is going to win Hero at the party tonight, and then he's going to give her to Claudio.'

'Claudio!' Don John said impatiently. 'I hate that young man. Here I am always in disgrace, [2] and Claudio is my brother's favourite. I wish I could do something that would damage Claudio.' He looked at Conrad and Borachio angrily. 'Will you two help me?'

Conrad and Borachio bowed deeply. They knew that Don John was always plotting against somebody.

---

1. **plotting** : making a secret plan to harm a person.
2. **in disgrace** : state in which other people do not respect you because you have behaved badly.

Go back to the text

1 Indicate whether the following statements are true (T) or false (F), and then correct the false ones.

		T	F
a.	Claudio has been in love with Hero since he first saw her.	☐	☐
b.	Don Pedro thinks that Hero is the right woman for Claudio.	☐	☐
c.	Don Pedro wishes to help Claudio win Hero's love.	☐	☐
d.	Don Pedro is going to have a big party at his house.	☐	☐
e.	All the guests at the party will have masks on.	☐	☐
f.	Don Pedro is going to tell Hero that Claudio loves her.	☐	☐
g.	Don Pedro is really in love with Hero.	☐	☐
h.	Don John doesn't like his brother Don Pedro.	☐	☐
i.	Don John is happy for Claudio and wishes to help him.	☐	☐

....

....

....

....

....

Although most of Leonato's guests were looking forward to the party...

Although and however

Although and *however* are both used to join contrasting ideas.

Below are five different ways of expressing the same pair of contrasting ideas. Instead of using *but* we can use *although* or *however*. Be careful of the punctuation!

Claudio loves Hero very much, **but** *he is afraid to tell her.*
Although *Claudio loves Hero very much, he is afraid to tell her.*
Claudio is afraid to tell her, **although** *he loves her very much.*
Claudio loves Hero very much. **However,** *he is afraid to tell her.*
Claudio loves Hero very much. He is, **however,** *afraid to tell her.*

2 Join the sentences below using *although* and *however*.

Example: Don John is Don Pedro's brother. Don John hates him.

Although Don John is Don Pedro's brother, Don John hates him.
Don John is Don Pedro's brother. However, Don John hates him.

a. Beatrice is a funny, beautiful young woman. Benedick doesn't like her.

....

....

b. I much prefer Hero. Beatrice is certainly a splendid young woman.

....

....

c. Beatrice says that a friend is like a hat for Benedick. Benedick is a good and faithful friend.

....

....

d. Claudio is going to marry Hero. Claudio has always said that he doesn't want to get married.

....

....

e. Benedick will fall in love someday. Benedick says that he will never surrender to one woman.

....

....

f. It is really Claudio who is in love with Hero. Antonio thinks that the Prince is in love with Hero.

....

....

g. I am Don Pedro's brother. He prefers Claudio to me.

....

....

h. Don John has plotted against his brother before. They are friends now.

....

....

Getting it down on paper

3 Complete the sentences of this summary of Chapter Two with the missing words or phrases.

Claudio liked Hero when he saw her before the war, but [1]...........*now*........... that he has seen her again he loves her.
Although [2].., he doesn't have the courage to speak to her directly.
When the Prince hears about Claudio's problem, he [3]...
.... and Claudio accepts the Prince's offer.
However, a servant [4]..., and tells Antonio [5]................................ .
Then Antonio tells Leonato and Leonato decides to [6]................................ Hero so that she will know what to do.
Someone else is following the courtship of Hero: it is Don John.
Don John is [7]... . He hates Claudio because [8]... . So Don John, with the help of his two friends, wants to [9]... .

Before you read

1 **Listen to Chapter Three twice.**
The first time you listen complete the following sentences with the missing words.
The second time you listen indicate who says the sentences: *Beatrice, Claudio, Benedick, Don Pedro, Hero* or *Don John.*

a. 'A man ....*without*.......... a ....*beard*.......... is too
young for me.'   ....*Beatrice*..........

b. 'I'll .... with you if you are
.........................., and if you don't talk too much.'   ....

c. 'I want to .... about love.'   ....

d. 'Benedick? .... Benedick?'   ....

e. 'He thinks he's very ...., but everyone
.... him, really.'   ....

f. 'I don't like the .... – I don't like it at
....'   ....

g. 'So the Prince has .... me.'   ....

h. 'What a .... girl she is – I hate her.'   ....

CHAPTER THREE

Voices behind Masks

here was a grand dinner in the hall of Leonato's house before the party. Everybody ate and drank well, and there was music and laughter.

'Is Don John here?' Leonato asked Antonio. 'I haven't seen him.'

'What an angry man he is!' Beatrice commented. 'He just sits there, he never says anything at all. Still,' she went on, 'he's not like Benedick – that one talks far too much. Really, uncle,' she joked, 'a perfect man would be half like Benedick and half like Don John!'

'I hope you find a man like that one day,' Leonato told her kindly. 'I'd like to see you married, Beatrice.'

'I'll never marry, uncle,' Beatrice replied. 'I don't like beards.' [1]

Her uncle laughed.

1. **beards :**

'What's wrong with a man with a beard?' he asked.

'A man with a beard is too old for me,' Beatrice said.

'What if the man you marry doesn't have a beard, Beatrice?' he asked.

'Impossible!' Beatrice replied sharply. 'A man without a beard is too young for me.'

Antonio turned to Hero. He was thinking about the offer of marriage that he was sure Don Pedro would make her at the party.

'You'll do as your father wants, I hope?' he asked her gently.

'Of course she will!' Beatrice interrupted. 'Hero will do her duty. She'll always say, "as you wish, father," it's her nature.' She paused for a moment. 'But if the man is ugly, Hero, you should refuse him, and say, "as I wish, father." That's what I would do!' she said defiantly. [1]

When dinner was finished, everyone went to change for the dance. They put on masks, and splendid costumes, and then came back into the main hall. The servants had removed the tables, and there was now space for dancing.

Don Pedro approached Hero.

'Will you walk with me?' he asked her tenderly. 'I have something to tell you.'

'I'll walk with you if you are handsome, and if you don't talk too much,' Hero told him.

'I want to talk about love,' Don Pedro said gently. He led her away from the other people in the hall.

Soon everyone was involved in exciting conversations.

Don Pedro's servant, Balthazar, was also wearing a mask. Balthazar was in love with Margaret, one of Hero's ladies-in-waiting. [2] He came up to Margaret and began to speak to her.

'I wish you liked me,' he began.

'It's a good thing for you that I don't like you,' Margaret replied. 'You see,' she joked, 'I have a lot of bad qualities.'

1. **defiantly** : in a way that shows resistance or disobedience.
2. **ladies-in-waiting** : high-ranking servants.

'Bad qualities,' Balthazar repeated. 'What are they?'

'I say my prayers out loud,' Margaret told him.

'I loved you before you told me that,' Balthazar said, 'but now I love you even more. Anyone who hears you pray can say, "amen".'

Benedick decided to punish Beatrice for her rudeness. He came up to her in his mask.

'Someone told me that you're not really witty [1] at all,' he said. 'You get all of your jokes from books – that's what this person said.'

'I bet it was Benedick who said that,' Beatrice replied. 'He doesn't like me at all – it's just the kind of thing Benedick would say about me!'

Benedick was enjoying himself. He could see that Beatrice was angry.

'Benedick?' he asked her. 'Who's Benedick?'

'Surely you know who Benedick is?' Beatrice said.

'I don't know him,' Benedick insisted. 'Who is he?'

'Oh, he's Don Pedro's clown,' [2] Beatrice said angrily. 'He's a fool really, and not funny at all. He just says rude things about everyone, and that makes fools laugh. If people don't laugh at what he says, he gets very unhappy. He thinks he's very clever, but everyone hates him, really.'

The music and dancing went on until very late in the night. At last it was over, and the masked figures began to leave the great hall.

Don John had been watching the dancers with his friends Conrad and Borachio. Don John had seen Don Pedro talking to Hero. He was sure that the Prince was in love with her. He looked gloomily [3] at the few people who were still in the hall. Then he saw a man's figure. He recognised Claudio.

'You're Benedick, aren't you?' he asked.

'I am,' the man replied.

'You're a friend of my brother the Prince,' Don John said. 'Please tell him that he cannot marry Hero. She does not come from a noble family.'

1. **witty** : funny.
2. **clown** : a person who acts in a funny or foolish way.
3. **gloomily** : unhappily.

Voices behind Masks

'Marry her?' the masked man said. 'What makes you think Don Pedro wants to marry Hero?'

'I heard them talking,' Don John replied. 'He told her he loves her. I don't like the news – I don't like it at all!'

Don John walked away with Conrad and Borachio.

Claudio leant against the wall.

'So the Prince has tricked [1] me,' he thought angrily. 'He was only pretending to win Hero for me – now he has won her for himself!'

Benedick came into the hall. He was looking for his friend.

'You've heard the news?' he asked. 'The Prince has stolen Hero from you, Claudio!'

Claudio groaned [2] loudly.

'Leave me alone, Benedick, just leave me alone!' he cried.

Benedick turned to leave his friend. His own thoughts were not happy ones.

'She said I was Don Pedro's clown,' he thought. 'Do people really call me that? Do they call me that because they think I'm stupid, or because they think I'm witty? Or was it something that Beatrice just invented? Perhaps they don't call me that at all!' he thought. 'What a horrible girl she is – I hate her!'

---

1. **tricked** : deceived.
2. **groaned** : made a noise indicating pain or suffering.

Go back to the text

- - - - - - - **FCE** - - - - - - -

1 Rewrite the following sentences from the text using the words given.

Example: 'A man with a beard is too old for me ...... A man without a beard is too young for me.'
MARRY
Beatrice means *that she doesn't want to marry any man.*

a. 'You'll do as your father wants, I hope.'
WHAT
I hope ....

b. 'She'll always say, "as you wish father".'
OBEY
She ....

c. 'It's a good thing for you that I don't like you,' Margaret replied. 'You see,' she joked, 'I have a lot of bad qualities.'
BECAUSE
You are lucky ....

d. 'Someone told me that you're not really witty at all. You get all of your jokes from books.'
HAVE TO
Since you are not ....

e. 'He thinks he's very clever, but everyone hates him really.'
ALTHOUGH
Everyone ....

f. 'She does not come from a noble family.'
NOT
Her family ....

He looked gloomily at the few people who were still in the hall.

Defining relative clauses

The part of the sentence beginning with *who* is called a defining relative clause.

*Don John looked gloomily at the few people **who** were still in the hall.*

This kind of relative clause identifies or defines the person or thing we are talking about and so it is called a defining relative clause.
Defining clauses can begin with *who* (when we are talking about people), *which* (when we are talking about things) and *that* (when were talking about either people or things).

Look at the following examples.

a. *William Shakespeare is the playwright* **who wrote** Much Ado About Nothing.

b. *Michael Keaton is the actor* **that played Dogberry in the film version of Much Ado About Nothing.**

c. Much Ado About Nothing *is the play by Shakespeare* **which always makes me laugh the most.**

We can also write sentences d), e), f) and g) without *that*, *whom* and *which* because they are the objects of the verbs in the relative clause.

d. *Don John is the character* **(that)** *I hate the most.*

e. *Hero is the character* **(whom)** *I like the most.*

f. *Romeo and Juliet is the play by Shakespeare* **(which)** *most people know best.*

g. *Michael Keaton is the actor* **(that)** *I saw at a party in Hollywood.*

2 **Join a sentence from column A with a sentence from column B using a relative clause with *who*, *which* or *that*, omitting the relative pronoun where possible.**

Example: Shakespeare is the famous poet who wrote Much Ado About Nothing.
(This sentence can't be rewritten without the relative pronoun because it is the subject of the verb)

A.

1. Shakespeare is the famous poet.
2. The messenger gave Leonato a letter.
3. Don Pedro has a plan.
4. Everybody wore masks at the party.
5. Benedick is the man.
6. Don John has a plan.
7. Beatrice is a young woman.
8. Hero is the young woman.

B.

a. It will ruin Claudio.
b. Claudio wants to marry her.
c. It will help Claudio win Hero.
d. Beatrice likes to make fun of him.
e. She is always making jokes.
f. It said that the Prince of Aragon, Don Pedro, was coming for a visit.
g. Leonato gave it at his house.
h. He wrote *Much Ado About Nothing*.

....
....
....
....
....
....
....

The opposite of what they seem

3 In this play many things are the opposite of what they seem, and the same is true in this crossword puzzle where the clues given are the opposite of the word to write in the squares. The number in brackets refers to the page where you can find the word.

Across

5. Nephew. (17)
8. Smiled. (20)
10. Merrily. (36)
12. Warm appreciation. (20)
13. Walk hurriedly. (25)
14. Polite. (18)
16. Boys have smooth faces, and men have .... . (32)
18. Son. (17)
19. Gloomily. (27)

Down

1. Hated. (36)
2. Not humorous. (36)
3. Raise yourself. (17)
4. Slowly. (18)
6. Stupid. (36)
7. Treated honestly. (37)
9. Words full of logical meaning. (26)
11. Made a joyous sound. (37)
15. Merry. (20)
17. It might not be that way. It only .... to be that way. (18)

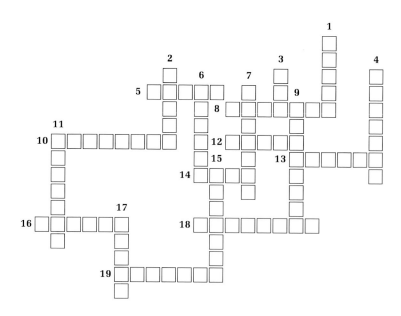

Summing it all up

FCE

4 Below is a summary of the first three chapters, but you must put the paragraphs in the right order.
Then choose the best title from the list below for each paragraph.

a. Victors in War. Losers in Love.
b. A Prince Goes Courting ... for a Friend.
c. Good News
d. A Woman that Stings Like a Bee
e. The Cowardly Lover
f. Love is Here to Stay

[1] [c.] Leonato, the Governor of Messina, was strolling through the city when he received a letter. The letter said that Don Pedro, the Prince of Aragon was coming for a visit. Don Pedro had just won an important battle, and since he had lost few men, everyone was in a festive mood.

[ ] That evening at the party, Don Pedro went to Hero and pretended to be Claudio; he said that he loved her. All would have been fine except that Don Pedro's brother Don John had seen him talking with Hero, and Don John hated his brother.

[ ] Unfortunately, Claudio was afraid to declare his love to Hero. However, Don Pedro had an idea. That night there was going to be a masked party at Leonato's. Don Pedro would pretend that he was Claudio and go and talk to Hero.

[ ] Later, Don Pedro arrived with the two young noblemen Benedick and Claudio. Benedick immediately began to exchange sarcastic remarks with Beatrice, but Claudio was busy thinking. Indeed, Claudio now knew that Hero was the woman for him, and he decided that he wanted to marry her.

[ ] So, later when Don John recognized Claudio, he told him that Don Pedro wanted to marry Hero. Claudio became very upset, but he wasn't alone. His friend Benedick had talked to Beatrice at the party. He was also pretending to be somebody else. Beatrice had told Benedick that everybody thought he was a fool. Benedick was now wondering whether Beatrice had told him the truth or not.

[ ] Leonato had a beautiful daughter named Hero, and a very spirited and witty niece named Beatrice. Beatrice wanted to know if a certain Florentine nobleman named Benedick had survived the battle. In her own way Beatrice was happy when she discovered that he was still alive because she took great pleasure in making fun of him.

Tragic and Comic Elements in *Much Ado About Nothing*

Although *Much Ado About Nothing* is undoubtedly a comedy, many critics have commented on the tragedy in the play. An interesting comparison can be made between this play and *Romeo and Juliet*, where the tragic elements dominate. [1] The key feature of the plot in both plays concerns the intervention of a friar in a young couple's love. In *Romeo and Juliet* the friar tries to help the lovers by giving Juliet a drug that will simulate [2] death. Tragedy occurs when a letter goes astray. [3] Romeo commits suicide when he thinks that Juliet is dead. She wakes up, sees his body, and kills herself.

In *Much Ado About Nothing* the friar's intention to help Hero also concerns the fiction that she is dead. In this play, however, there is no expectation of a tragic outcome. Borachio and Conrad may have been successful in persuading Claudio and Don Pedro that Hero has a lover, but the plot has no chance of success because Dogberry and the constables arrest Borachio and Conrad, and the audience knows that the truth will soon be discovered.

Dogberry and his colleagues are a source of English comedy in the play. They are in the same tradition as Bottom in *A Midsummer Night's Dream*. They are enthusiastic, naive, and their language is an absurd [4] mixture of pretension [5] and error. Despite their failings, however, they uncover [6] the truth of the plot.

Scene from the film Much Ado About Nothing *by Kenneth Branagh.*

1. **dominate** : are the most important feature of something.
2. **simulate** : create the effect or appearance of something else.
3. **goes astray** : becomes lost.
4. **absurd** : that should be laughed at.
5. **pretension** : claim to merit or importance.
6. **uncover** : find out.

One of the important themes of the play is that love can be created and destroyed by very trivial [1] forces, such as gossip and misunderstanding. This theme also contributes to the dominance of comic elements over tragic. The characters *in Much Ado About Nothing* fall in and out of love with each other as a result of what they hear from other people. Hero, for example, falls in love with Claudio because of what Don Pedro says to her when he is in disguise at the masked dance. Claudio falls out of love with Hero because of what he has heard about her disloyalty from Don John, and what he thinks he sees when he is outside her bedroom window.

Benedick and Beatrice fall in love because of Don Pedro's plot – they listen to conversations in which they seem to learn that they are loved by the other. In this play, plans and plots become the basis of real love. Benedick and Beatrice may have been the victims of Don Pedro's plot to make them fall in love, but the plot has enabled them to discover what they really feel for each other. This is the real point of the poem that Benedick writes to Beatrice, and Beatrice's letter to Benedick. His comment 'our hands against our hearts' shows that their actions are those of love, even if they do not realise they love each other.

1 **Answer the following questions.**

    a. What are the similarities between *Romeo and Juliet* and *Much Ado About Nothing*?

    ....

    b. What are the differences?

    ....

    c. How does the staged death end in *Romeo and Juliet*?

    ....

    d. What kind of character is Dogberry?

    ....

    e. What does *Much Ado About Nothing* say about love?

    ....

    f. What does Benedick mean when he says 'our hands against our hearts'?

    ....

1. **trivial** : unimportant.

Before you read

FCE

1 Listen to the first part of Chapter Four and say whether the following sentences are true (T) or false (F). Then read the text and correct the false ones.

		T	F
a.	Leonato has given Claudio permission to marry Hero.	☐	☐
b.	Benedick can't stand Hero.	☐	☐
c.	Beatrice is happy for Claudio and Hero.	☐	☐
d.	Benedick leaves the room because he doesn't want to talk to Hero.	☐	☐
e.	Claudio is very impatient to be married.	☐	☐
f.	The Prince is joking when he says that he will arrange a wedding between Benedick and Beatrice.	☐	☐
g.	Claudio has a plan to arrange a wedding between Beatrice and Benedick.	☐	☐

....

....

....

....

....

CHAPTER FOUR

Two Brothers, Two Plans

enedick was walking out of the hall when he met Don Pedro. The Prince asked him where Claudio was. 'He's in the hall, sir,' Benedick said coldly. 'He's very upset [1] about what's happened. You shouldn't have stolen Hero from him.'

'Stolen Hero? I haven't stolen Hero from Claudio,' Don Pedro said. 'I've just asked Leonato if Claudio can marry her! By the way, Benedick,' he went on, 'Beatrice is angry with you. What's all that about?'

'It's a silly business, sir,' Benedick said. 'That girl is always so rude to me – I can't stand [2] her!'

---

1. **upset** : unhappy.
2. **can't stand** : am not able to bear.

Much Ado About Nothing

2 Soon they could hear happy voices and laughter from the hall. Claudio came out holding Hero by the hand. Beatrice and Leonato were with them.

'You see, Benedick,' the Prince said happily, 'I told you the truth. Leonato has said that Claudio and Hero can be married. Now do you believe that I'm Claudio's friend?'

'Yes, I believe you,' replied Benedick, 'but please excuse me now. I don't want to talk to Beatrice.' He left the room.

3 The Prince turned to Claudio with a big smile. 'What do you say, my young friend? I won Hero for you, didn't I?'

Claudio blushed. [1]

'I'm so happy that I don't know what to say,' he began. 'I...'

'You say something then, Hero,' Beatrice interrupted. 'Or better still, just kiss him – then neither of you has to say anything!'

4 Suddenly she looked serious.

'Everyone is getting married except me,' she said quietly.

'I'll find you a husband,' Don Pedro offered.

Beatrice laughed.

'Thank you, sir, but I'll never marry,' she replied. She turned to Claudio and Hero. 'Congratulations to you both,' she said kindly. 'I'm happy for you.'

5 Leonato signalled to Beatrice to leave them. Beatrice bowed to the Prince and left.

Don Pedro was very pleased with himself. He had promised Claudio that he would win Hero for him, and he had succeeded. Now he began to wonder [2] if he could not find a husband for Beatrice as well.

'Well, my friend, you'll be a married man one week from now,' he remarked.

'It'll be the longest week of my life,' Claudio said. 'I wish the wedding were tomorrow!'

---

1. **blushed** : went red in the face.
2. **wonder** : ask himself.

Two Brothers, Two Plans

Suddenly an idea occurred to Don Pedro.

'I know you're impatient to be married,' he said to Claudio and Hero. 'But we'll make this week a very pleasant one for you both, I promise. I'm going to arrange another wedding – between Beatrice and Benedick!'

Everybody laughed. They thought the Prince was joking.

Don Pedro held up his hand.

'No, I'm serious,' he told them all. 'I think I can do it. But I shall need your help. What do you say, Leonato – will you help me to arrange it?'

'I'll do everything I can,' Leonato said. 'But I don't see how you'll manage [1] it, sir. Benedick and Beatrice hate each other!'

'What about you, Claudio – will you help me?' the Prince asked.

'Of course I will,' Claudio replied.

'And you, Hero? Will you help as well?' Don Pedro asked.

'I'll do everything I can to get a good husband for Beatrice,' Hero told him.

'A good husband,' Don Pedro said thoughtfully. 'I think Benedick will be a good husband for Beatrice, you know. This is what we'll do,' he said excitedly.

The Prince began to explain his plan.

The Prince's brother, Don John, was also busy with plans of his own. He knew now that it was Claudio who was going to marry Hero, and not the Prince. Don John decided to spoil [2] the wedding because he wanted to hurt his brother and Claudio. He discussed the matter with Borachio.

'I've got an idea, sir!' Borachio said excitedly. 'I think I know how we can spoil this wedding.'

'Well, what is it?' Don John asked impatiently. 'What are we going to do?'

---

1. **manage** : succeed in doing something.
2. **spoil** : ruin.

8

Borachio explained that he was very close to Margaret, Hero's lady-in-waiting.

'Very close, sir, if you understand me,' he said with a smile. 'Close enough to go to her bedroom at night!'

'What does that matter?' Don John wanted to know. 'How can that help us?'

'It's very easy to go from Margaret's room to Hero's,' Borachio said with a smile.

'I still don't understand what you mean,' Don John told him. 'What are you going to do?'

Borachio explained his plan.

'Don Pedro thinks that Hero is a beautiful and honourable girl. Go and tell him that you have discovered that she is not honourable at all, sir. Tell the Prince that Hero has a secret lover – me! Say that you can prove it. Wait until it's late at night. Make Claudio and Don Pedro stand under Hero's bedroom window. I will then stand at the window. I'll talk to Margaret as if she were Hero – and Margaret will seem to be Hero. Don't you see, sir?' he asked excitedly. 'The Prince and Claudio will think Hero is in love with me – Claudio will call off [1] the wedding!'

'What about Hero?' Don John asked. 'What if she hears you and Margaret talking?'

'Don't worry, sir,' Borachio promised. 'I'll make sure that she isn't in her room that night.'

'It might just work!' Don John said quietly. 'Let's try your plan, Borachio. If it works, I'll give you a thousand ducats.' [2]

---

1. **call off** : cancel.
2. **ducats** : gold coins that were used in the past.

Go back to the text

1 Chapter Four has been divided into eight sections. Choose the best title for each section.

   a. Benedick's Confusion

   b. Lovers United

   c. Time Will Tell

   d. Sealed With a Kiss

   e. Beatrice, the Odd Woman Out

   f. A Game for a Long, Slow Week

   g. Friends Plot to Help Friends

   h. The Man Who Hated Weddings

   i. A Sinister [1] Case of Mistaken Identity

'You shouldn't have stolen Hero from him.'

Should

Look at these two sentences and the explanations which follow.

The basic idea of both is the same, except that (a) is in the present and (b) is in the past.

a. *You **shouldn't steal** Hero from him* = It is not a good thing for you to steal Hero from him.

b. *You **shouldn't have stolen** Hero from him* = It was not a good thing for you to steal Hero from him.

or

a. *Benedick **should marry** Beatrice* = It is a good thing for Benedick to marry Beatrice.

b. *Benedick **should have married** Beatrice* = It was a good thing for Benedick to marry Beatrice, but he didn't.

The basic structure in the past is:

Subject + *should* (or *shouldn't*) + *have* + *past participle of verb*.

---

1. **sinister** : frightening.

2 Choose the correct verb from the box to complete the sentence, using the past of *should*. Some verbs can be used more than once.

Example: Claudio .shouldn't have been. angry with Don Pedro.

trust   try   be   doubt   talk

a. Beatrice .... so rude to Benedick.

b. Benedick .... to trick Beatrice at the party.

c. Don Pedro .... more quietly to Hero.

d. Claudio .... Hero.

e. Nobody .... Don John.

f. Benedick .... that Don Pedro was really Claudio's friend.

'I won Hero for you, didn't I?'

Question tags

Questions tags have numerous uses in English.

- *I won Hero for you, **didn't I**?* – The speaker is asking the other person to agree with him.
- *Don John didn't really try to ruin the wedding, **did he**?* – The speaker is expressing surprise.
- *That's Beatrice over there, **isn't it**?* – The speaker is asking the other person for confirmation of the information – the speaker is checking a fact.

Questions tags use the same auxiliary verbs or inversion as regular questions; the main difference is that the main verb (except with the verb 'to be') does not appear. If the main sentence is affirmative, the question tag is negative, and vice versa. Finally, when the question tag is negative, the contracted form of the verb is generally used.

- *You saw the film, **didn't you**?*

3 For each sentence and question tag indicate which tense is being used.

A. **Affirmative sentences – Negative question tags**

1. *Much Ado About Nothing* has got a happy ending, <u>hasn't it?</u>   ....
2. You would marry her, <u>wouldn't you?</u>   ....
3. You are going to Messina tomorrow, <u>aren't you?</u>   ....
4. You like dancing, <u>don't you?</u>   ....
5. Shakespeare wrote *Much Ado About Nothing*, <u>didn't he?</u>   ....
6. Don Pedro has arrived, <u>hasn't he?</u>   ....
7. She's from Florence, <u>isn't she?</u>   ....
8. There are two gentlemen from Verona here, <u>aren't there?</u>   ....

B. Negative sentences – Affirmative question tags

1. You aren't going to fight Claudio, <u>are you?</u> ....
2. There isn't much to do, <u>is there?</u> ....
3. Hero hasn't really betrayed Claudio, <u>has she?</u> ....
4. You don't like that woman, <u>do you?</u> ....
5. Don Pedro didn't ask Hero to get married, <u>did he?</u> ....
6. You wouldn't marry her, <u>would you?</u> ....
7. You haven't got a light, <u>have you?</u> ....
8. He isn't very intelligent, <u>is he?</u>* ....

* Notice the irregularity with the 1st-person singular of the verb to be.
I am the man you love, aren't I? (aren't I = am I not).

4 **A. Match the question tags with the sentences.**

don't they?	did he?	haven't they?	will you?
won't you?	wasn't there?	was there?	didn't he?

1. Shakespeare wrote many comedies, ...
2. There was a man outside Hero's window, ...
3. He didn't really do that, ...
4. You will help me, ...
5. There wasn't a constable there, ...
6. You won't ever get married, ...
7. They have beautiful masks, ...
8. They have got a beautiful house, ...

B. Now add questions tags to following sentences.

1. Benedick was walking out of the hall when he met Don Pedro, ... ?
2. Claudio came out holding Hero by the hand, ... ?
3. I am the only one not getting married, ... ?
4. Don Pedro was very pleased with himself, ... ?
5. Don John doesn't like his brother, ... ?
6. Hero would never betray Claudio, ... ? (A sentence with 'never' is considered a negative sentence, so it takes an affirmative question tag).
7. She didn't really have a lover, ... ?
8. This is the end of this exercise, ... ?

Before you read

FCE

1 Read the passage carefully. Some of the lines are correct and some have a word which is incorrect. If a line is correct, put a tick (✔) in the space. If a line is incorrect, write the word in the space. Then listen and check.

Benedick was walking in Leonato's garden. ....✔...............

He was thinking all about his friend Claudio. ...._all_...............

1. 'He's certainly very different now that he's in love with Hero,' he told to himself. ....

2. 'Claudio and I used to be very much similar. ....

3. We used to laugh at men who fell over in love. Now look at him! ....

4. He's lost his interest in the army, all he cares about is Hero and what she thinks!' ....

5. Benedick had shook his head impatiently. ....

6. 'No,' he told himself, 'I like women, but I'll not never fall in love with one. ....

7. That's for sure!' ....

8. Just then he saw the Prince and a group of men come all into the garden. One of the men was Claudio. ....

9. 'The great lover!' Benedick laughed to himself. 'I'll hide myself here, ...

10. and hear what Claudio and the Prince are being talking about' ....

11. The Prince, however, had already seen Benedick in the garden. ....

12. He touched Claudio on the his arm, and pointed to where Benedick was hiding. ....

13. 'Remember my plan to make Benedick fall in love with Beatrice,' he said softly. ....

14. Don Pedro called Balthazar loudly. 'Let's have some music, my friend,' he commanded. ....

15. 'I want to hear to that song you were singing before.' ....

CHAPTER ✦ FIVE

Benedick and Beatrice in the Garden

enedick was walking in Leonato's garden. He was thinking about his friend Claudio.

'He's certainly very different now that he's in love with Hero,' he told himself. 'Claudio and I used to be very similar. We used to laugh at men who fell in love. Now look at him! He's lost his interest in the army, all he cares about is Hero and what she thinks!'

Benedick shook his head impatiently.

'No,' he told himself, 'I like women, but I'll never fall in love with one. That's for sure!'

Just then he saw the Prince and a group of men coming into the garden. One of the men was Claudio.

Benedick and Beatrice in the Garden

'The great lover!' Benedick laughed to himself. 'I'll hide here, and hear what Claudio and the Prince are talking about.'

The Prince, however, had already seen Benedick in the garden. He touched Claudio on the arm, and pointed to where Benedick was hiding.

'Remember my plan to make Benedick fall in love with Beatrice,' he said softly. [1]

Don Pedro called Balthazar loudly.

'Let's have some music, my friend,' he commanded. 'I want to hear that song you were singing before.'

Balthazar stepped forward. The musicians began to play, and Balthazar started to sing. His song was about love. The song suggested that women should not trust men – all men were liars about love.

'Sigh [2] no more, ladies, sigh no more,
Men were deceivers [3] ever; [4]
One foot in sea, one foot on shore,
To one thing constant [5] never.
Then sigh not so,
But let them go,
And you be blithe [6] and bonny, [7]
Converting all your sounds of woe [8]
Into hey nonny, nonny.'

---

1. **softly** : very quietly.
2. **sigh** : make a noise indicating sadness.
3. **deceivers** : liars (in matters of love).
4. **ever** : always.
5. **constant** : faithful.
6. **blithe** : cheerful.
7. **bonny** : happy.
8. **woe** : suffering.

Much Ado About Nothing

Everyone applauded [1] when the song was finished.

'That was a good song, my friend,' Don Pedro told Balthazar. 'Remember that we shall want some good songs tomorrow night. We're all going to sing outside Hero's bedroom window.'

'I shall do my best,' Balthazar replied politely. He bowed to the Prince and walked back to the house with the musicians.

Don Pedro waited until Balthazar and the musicians were out of sight. Then he looked at the place where Benedick was hiding, and winked [2] at Claudio. Claudio smiled back at him.

The Prince began to speak in a loud voice to Leonato.

'What was that you were saying before?' he asked. 'Something about Beatrice being in love with Benedick?'

Leonato winked back at Claudio and Don Pedro before he replied.

'It's true, sir,' he said very seriously. 'I can hardly [3] believe it myself. Beatrice has always been rude to Benedick – but she loves him, there's no doubt about that.'

'Perhaps she's just pretending to be in love,' Don Pedro said. 'What makes you think she's really in love?'

'She told you all about it, didn't she?' Leonato said to Claudio. 'Did you think she was pretending?'

'She's really in love,' Claudio replied. 'The poor girl loves Benedick desperately, she told me herself. But she'll never say anything to him. She can't tell him, you see, because she's always been so rude to him. She thinks Benedick would just laugh at her.'

'She's even tried writing a letter to tell him what she feels,' Leonato said. 'But she didn't send it. She tore the letter up. Poor girl, she's suffering very badly!'

---

1. **applauded** :

2. **winked** : closed one eye quickly as a signal to someone.

3. **hardly** : almost not.

Benedick and Beatrice in the Garden

Don Pedro was very pleased at the way his plan was going. He found it difficult not to laugh. He controlled himself, however.

'Why don't we tell Benedick that Beatrice is in love with him?' he suggested. 'Perhaps we could help Beatrice by letting him know.'

'No, no, you mustn't do that!' Claudio interrupted. 'It would do Beatrice no good. Benedick would just laugh at her. We mustn't say anything, sir.'

The men stayed in the garden for a while longer, and then they all went back into the house.

Benedick remained [1] in the garden by himself. He was very surprised at what he had heard. He began to think about Beatrice in a new way.

'It's true she's a beautiful girl,' he told himself. 'She's also a very honourable girl, there's no doubt about that. They say she loves me.'

His ideas about Beatrice began to change.

'Perhaps I've been wrong about her,' he thought. 'She's a lovely girl, after all!'

He began to walk slowly back to the house. He was very thoughtful.

Suddenly, he saw Beatrice in the garden. He was pleased to see her, and he smiled at her.

'I've been sent to look for you,' Beatrice told him coldly. 'Dinner is ready, and everyone is waiting for you.'

Benedick decided to be very polite to Beatrice now that he thought she loved him.

'Thank you for the trouble [2] you have taken to find me,' he said courteously. [3]

'Trouble?' Beatrice repeated. 'It was no trouble to come and look for you.'

1. **remained** : stayed.
2. **trouble** : effort.
3. **courteously** : politely.

'If it was no trouble, perhaps it was a pleasure to come and look for me?' Benedick asked gently.

'What makes you think it was a pleasure?' Beatrice replied angrily. She walked away from Benedick.

Benedick followed her into the house.

'There's no doubt about it,' he thought. 'She's in love with me, all right. She said it was "no trouble" to come and look for me. She really does love me!'

The first part of Don Pedro's plan had gone well. Benedick was sure that Beatrice loved him, and he was beginning to look at her in a different way.

Now it was Hero's turn to persuade Beatrice that Benedick loved her. She went into the garden with her two ladies-in-waiting, Ursula and Margaret. She sent Margaret to look for Beatrice.

'Tell her that we're talking about her,' Hero ordered Margaret. 'Tell her to come and listen to what we say.'

Margaret went back into the house, and soon Beatrice came into the garden. Beatrice approached Hero and Ursula carefully, so that she would not be seen. She listened to the conversation of the two girls. At first she could not believe what she was hearing.

'So you see,' Hero was saying to Ursula, 'poor Benedick is terribly [1] in love with Beatrice.'

'Are you sure about that?' Ursula asked. 'I thought that Benedick did not like Beatrice at all.'

'It's true,' Hero told her. 'Claudio and the Prince told me all about it. They asked me to talk to Beatrice, but I said it would do no good. Beatrice is very proud, and she would just laugh at poor Benedick.'

'You're probably right,' Ursula agreed. Then she went on in a loud

1. **terribly** : very much.

voice. 'Beatrice is so proud that she can't love anyone. It's better not to say anything to her about Benedick. She would just make the poor man suffer horribly with her cruelty and her jokes.'

'I'm going to talk to Benedick,' Hero said. 'I'm going to help him if I can. I'm going to tell him that he's far too good for Beatrice.'

Ursula sighed deeply.

'It's true that Benedick is a very handsome man,' she said softly. 'Many women would be happy if he fell in love with them.'

Ursula and Hero began to walk back to the house. They knew that Beatrice had been listening to their talk. They both wanted to laugh at the trick ¹ they had played on Beatrice, but they managed to look serious.

Beatrice was not pleased at what she had heard.

'My friends think I am too proud to love!' she told herself. 'They say Benedick loves me. They say he is a good man. Perhaps they're right – perhaps I should love Benedick!'

1. **trick** : joke.

Go back to the text

FCE

1 **Choose the best answers (a, b, c or d) for the following questions.**

1. How did Claudio used to react to men who were in love?
   - [ ] **a.** He used to be sad because he wanted to be in love.
   - [ ] **b.** He used to laugh at them.
   - [ ] **c.** He used to ignore them.
   - [ ] **d.** He used to wonder how it was possible to be in love with a woman.

2. How has Claudio changed?
   - [ ] **a.** He only thinks about what Hero thinks and he no longer cares about the army.
   - [ ] **b.** He no longer cares about what Hero thinks.
   - [ ] **c.** Now, he only wants to listen to love songs.
   - [ ] **d.** Now, he only wants to go to parties.

3. Why does Don Pedro wink at Claudio?
   - [ ] **a.** To let him know that they can begin talking about how Beatrice is in love with Benedick.
   - [ ] **b.** Because he likes Claudio.
   - [ ] **c.** To let him know that Benedick is hiding nearby.
   - [ ] **d.** To let him know that Benedick will believe them.

4. According to Claudio why doesn't Beatrice tell Benedick that she loves him?
   - [ ] **a.** Because she is still angry with him.
   - [ ] **b.** Because she is afraid, after all their fights, that he will make fun of her.
   - [ ] **c.** Because she herself is not sure that she is in love with him.
   - [ ] **d.** Because Beatrice is not from a noble family.

5. How does Benedick speak to Beatrice now that he thinks she is in love with him?
   - [ ] **a.** He is very polite and kind.
   - [ ] **b.** He is even ruder than usual.
   - [ ] **c.** He is timid.
   - [ ] **d.** He tries to be witty.

6. How does Beatrice react to Benedick?
   - [ ] **a.** She too is very polite and kind.
   - [ ] **b.** She speaks to him in a rude and abrupt manner.
   - [ ] **c.** She too becomes timid.
   - [ ] **d.** She is shocked.

'Beatrice is so proud that she can't love anyone.'

So and such

Look at these two sentences:

*Beatrice is **so** proud.*

*Beatrice is **such** a proud person.*

Here, both *so* and *such* make the adjective even stronger; the only difference is that *so* is used with just the adjective, while *such* is used with the adjective and the noun.

Often *so* and *such* are used before a result or consequence clause beginning with 'that'.

*Beatrice is **so** proud that she can't love anyone.*

*Beatrice is **such** a proud woman that she can't love anyone.*

2 Add *so* or *such* to the sentences in column A, and then combine them with the sentences in column B using the correct verb from the box in the correct tense.

Example: Beatrice's jokes about Benedick were **so** rude
that the messenger **was** shocked.

A.

1.   Beatrice's jokes about Benedick were .... rude.

2.   Claudio is .... timid.

3.   Don Pedro has made .... a good plan.

4.   Benedick tells .... funny stories.

5.   Don John is .... jealous.

6.   Balthazar sang .... a beautiful song.

7.   Claudio will be .... angry when he discovers that Hero has a secret lover.

B.   applaud   call off   decide   believe   laugh   ask

a. Benedick actually .... that Beatrice loves him.

b. He .... the wedding.

c. Everybody always ....

d. The messenger .... shocked.

e. He .... to ruin Claudio's wedding.

f. He .... Don Pedro to talk to Hero.

g. Everyone ....

62

Some extra information

Non-defining relative clauses

We have already looked at defining relative clauses (see page 38).
These clauses tell us specifically which person or thing we are talking about:
defining relative clauses are essential to the meaning of the sentence.
But there is another kind of relative clause, the non-defining relative clause:
it adds extra information.

Much Ado About Nothing, **which we saw five times**, *was written by William
Shakespeare.*

Here, the non-defining relative clause (**which we saw five times**) is not essential
to the meaning of the sentence, we know exactly which play the speaker is
talking about.

That is the play **which we saw five times**.

Here, without the defining relative clause (**which we saw five times**), we don't
know which play the speaker is talking about.

In addition, in non-defining clauses we only use *which* and *who* never *that.*
Which and *who* can never be omitted.
Finally, the non-defining relative clause is always separated from the rest of the
sentence by commas.

3 Add the extra information to make sentences with non-defining relative clauses.

> It takes place in Messina.   She is Hero's cousin.
> He has always sworn that he would never fall in love.
> ~~They were only published after the playwright's death.~~
> He is Don Pedro's brother.   He is a brave and capable soldier.

Example: Shakespeare's plays, which were only published after the playwright's
death, are often considered masterpieces of world literature.

a. ~~Shakespeare's plays are often considered masterpieces of world literature.~~

b. *Much Ado About Nothing* talks about the fragility of love.

c. Beatrice is always making witty remarks.

d. Don John plots to destroy the love between Claudio and Hero.

e. Claudio is afraid to declare his love to Hero.

f. Because of Don Pedro's clever plan Benedick is beginning to look at Beatrice
differently.

Before you read

1 Fill in the gaps in the text with the words given below. Then listen and check.

> short   journey   serious   right   make
> exchanged   explain   hair   want   jokes   place
> anything   don't   day   wedding

Later that ¹....................... the Prince and Leonato were talking to Claudio and
Benedick. 'I must go home after your ²......................., my friend,' Don Pedro told
Claudio. 'Then I will accompany you on the ³.......................,' Claudio offered.
'It's the least I can do after your kindness to me.' 'Nonsense!' the Prince replied.
'Your ⁴....................... is with your new wife. You don't want to go on a long
journey just after your wedding. No, I'll take Benedick with me. He's the man I
⁵....................... . The journey will be ⁶....................... once he starts telling his
⁷....................... and stories.' 'The truth is, I'm not as witty as I once was,'
Benedick admitted. 'I ⁸....................... know why it is.' Don Pedro and Claudio
⁹....................... a secret smile with each other. They knew why Benedick was
more ¹⁰....................... than he had been. They knew he was thinking about
Beatrice. 'You do look quite sad,' Claudio told his friend sympathetically.
'Is ¹¹....................... the matter?' 'It's just a toothache,' Benedick replied crossly.
'It'll pass.' 'Toothache?' Don Pedro said. 'I never knew that a toothache could
¹²....................... a man look sad, Benedick.' Benedick blushed fiercely. 'I think
he's in love,' Claudio said with a laugh. 'Look at the careful way he's dressed, and
the trouble he takes with his ¹³....................... – he's a man in love, I tell you!'
'You may be ¹⁴.......................,' Don Pedro agreed. 'That would ¹⁵.......................
why he looks so sad, as well.'

CHAPTER SIX

Benedick suffers for Love

ater that day the Prince and Leonato were talking to Claudio and Benedick.

'I must go home after your wedding, my friend,' Don Pedro told Claudio.

'Then I will accompany you on the journey,' Claudio offered. 'It's the least I can do after your kindness to me.'

'Nonsense!' the Prince replied. 'Your place is with your new wife. You don't want to go on a long journey just after your wedding. No, I'll take Benedick with me. He's the man I want. The journey will be short once he starts telling his jokes and stories.'

'The truth is, I'm not as witty as I once was,' Benedick admitted. 'I don't know why it is.'

Don Pedro and Claudio exchanged a secret smile with each other. They

knew why Benedick was more serious than he had been. They knew he was thinking about Beatrice.

'You do look quite sad,' Claudio told his friend sympathetically. 'Is anything the matter?'

'It's just a toothache,' Benedick replied crossly. [1] 'It'll pass.'

'Toothache?' Don Pedro said. 'I never knew that toothache could make a man look sad, Benedick.'

Benedick blushed fiercely. [2]

'I think he's in love,' Claudio said with a laugh. 'Look at the careful

1. **crossly** : angrily.
2. **blushed fiercely** : went very red in the face.

Benedick suffers for Love

way he's dressed, and the trouble he takes with his hair – he's a man in love, I tell you!'

'You may be right,' Don Pedro agreed. 'That would explain why he looks so sad, as well.'

Benedick did not enjoy his friends' jokes. He frowned for a moment, and then he suddenly turned to Leonato.

'Come with me, sir,' he said quickly. 'I have something important that I want to ask you.'

Leonato and Benedick walked away together.

'He's going to speak to Leonato!' Don Pedro said excitedly. 'He's going to ask for permission to marry Beatrice.'

There was a knock at the door, and Don John came into the room. He bowed politely to Claudio, and then spoke to his brother.

'I have something to tell you,' he said very seriously.

'Something to tell me?' the Prince repeated slowly. 'Is it something private, or can Claudio stay and hear?'

'What I have to say also concerns Claudio,' Don John replied. Now he spoke to Claudio. 'I know you are getting married tomorrow,' he said. 'My news is about Hero,' he went on. 'I've discovered that she is not an honourable girl – she has a lover!'

Don Pedro and Claudio were shocked by Don John's words. They did not know what to say. For a moment neither of them said anything.

'I know it's hard to believe,' Don John

continued, 'but I'm telling you the truth. I can prove that Hero is disloyal
to you. Come with me tonight, both of you. We'll stand outside Hero's
bedroom window – you'll see that what I've told you is the truth!'

'I can't believe it!' Claudio said angrily.

'Nor me!' Don Pedro agreed.

'I'm telling you the truth,' Don John said firmly. 'I don't want you to
make a terrible mistake, Claudio. You can't marry a girl who behaves like
Hero – she would dishonour [1] you!'

Claudio thought for a moment. He loved Hero, but he was also very
proud. He did not like the idea that Hero might be making a fool of him.
At last he made up his mind.

'Very well,' he told Don John, 'I'll come with you tonight. And if
you're right about Hero,' he decided angrily, 'I'll disgrace her at the
church tomorrow morning – I'll tell everyone what sort of girl she is!'

1. **dishonour** : bring shame on somebody.

Go back to the text

1 Choose the best answers (a, b, c or d) for the following questions.

1. Who is going to accompany Don Pedro on his journey home?
   - [ ] **a.** Benedick.
   - [ ] **b.** Claudio.
   - [ ] **c.** Leonato.
   - [ ] **d.** Beatrice.

2. Why does Don Pedro like travelling with Benedick?
   - [ ] **a.** Because Benedick knows how to fight and can, therefore, protect the Prince.
   - [ ] **b.** Because Benedick knows all the roads.
   - [ ] **c.** Because Benedick is a good horseman.
   - [ ] **d.** Because Benedick tells funny stories that make time pass more quickly.

3. Why doesn't Don Pedro think that Benedick really has a toothache?
   - [ ] **a.** Because Benedick has good teeth.
   - [ ] **b.** Because Benedick would have already gone to a dentist.
   - [ ] **c.** Because toothaches don't make men look sad.
   - [ ] **d.** Because Benedick eats without any difficulty.

4. Why does Benedick dress so well now?
   - [ ] **a.** Because he is in love.
   - [ ] **b.** Because he does not have to fight any wars, so he can now spend time on his clothing.
   - [ ] **c.** Because he likes dressing well for the Prince.
   - [ ] **d.** Because he is going to a masked ball.

5. What does Don John tell the Prince about Hero?
   - [ ] **a.** That she is really in love with the Prince.
   - [ ] **b.** That she is really in love with Benedick.
   - [ ] **c.** That she has a secret lover.
   - [ ] **d.** That she is already married.

6. How can Don John prove what he said is true?
   - [ ] **a.** He has some love letters written by Hero.
   - [ ] **b.** That night, he and the Prince will hide outside Hero's window.
   - [ ] **c.** He has some love poems written by Hero.
   - [ ] **d.** He has some letters that Hero's lover wrote to her.

'Since Hero is disloyal and would dishonour him, Claudio is going to disgrace her!'

Negative prefixes

Non, un and *dis* are the most common negative prefixes in English.

Non generally means the absence of a quality.

For example, *non-stop* means without a stop or pause and *nonsense* means the lack of sense or logical meaning.

Un generally makes a word mean its opposite.

Dis also generally makes a word mean its opposite.

However, you should generally check in your dictionary for the exact meaning.

2 Choose one of the words from the box and one of the three prefixes (*dis*, *un*, *non*) to complete the sentences. Check in your dictionary.

> loyal honour believe obedient aware
> like ~~trust~~ fiction

a. I ...distrust...... Don John because he has always plotted against me.

b. Beatrice tells Hero to be .... to her father if he tells her to marry an ugly man.

c. If you want to find books about science, you have to look in the .... section.

d. At the beginning of the play Beatrice .... Benedick very much, but then she falls in love with him.

e. When Hero went to get married in the church, she was totally .... that Claudio was suspicious of her.

f. In my opinion, Claudio and Don Pedro should have .... Don John when he told them that Hero had a secret lover.

g. Claudio believes that Hero has .... him by having a secret lover.

h. What would you do if you discover that your boyfriend was .... to you and had a secret lover?

Summing it all up

3 Below is a summary of Chapters 3-6, but four paragraphs (a, b, c and d) have been left out. Put them in the right place in the summary.

a. Unfortunately, Don Pedro was not the only one with a secret plan. Don John also had one, but his was meant to destroy Claudio's happiness. Don John was going to tell Claudio and Don Pedro that Hero had a secret lover, and that they should come that evening outside Hero's window and they would see Hero with her lover. The trick was that it would not be Hero, but Hero's lady-in-waiting Margaret dressed as Hero.

b. Benedick was very impressed by what he heard, and began to look at Beatrice differently. He began to admit that she was, after all, a very beautiful and honourable young woman. When Beatrice came to call him to come join the others, Benedick, for the first time, was polite to her. Beatrice, though, was still as rude as ever. Still, Benedick thought he could see in her words signs that she loved him.

c. So far then, Don Pedro's plan was a great success. In fact, Benedick began to act quite differently. He started to take special care with his dress and hair; and, what was more incredible, he no longer made jokes all the time. Of course, his friend Claudio noticed all this and made fun of him. Claudio's diagnosis was simple: Benedick was a man in love.

d. At first, Claudio was extremely upset because he thought that Don Pedro had tricked him. However, Don Pedro also went to Leonato, Hero's father, and arranged the marriage between Hero and Claudio. Claudio was then happy and could hardly wait to be married. The only problem now was that Benedick, Claudio's best friend, was depressed: Beatrice had told him that everyone thought that he was a fool. Beatrice also felt a little sad since her cousin was getting married and she wasn't.

Since Claudio was not brave enough to declare his love to Hero, Don Pedro volunteered to help him. At Leonato's masked party, Don Pedro pretended to be Claudio and spoke to Hero. He told her that he loved her. Unfortunately, Don John saw Don Pedro and Hero together. He then went to Claudio and told him that Don Pedro had stolen Hero from him.

Don Pedro, though, had a solution to all these problems: he had a plan to make Beatrice and Benedick fall in love with each other, and, at the same time, Claudio would enjoy himself the week before his wedding.

Before Don John carried out his plan, Don Pedro began his plan. He and Claudio walked in the garden near where Benedick was hiding. They knew that Benedick was there, but Benedick thought that they couldn't see him. So, Claudio and Don Pedro began to talk about how Beatrice was really in love with Benedick but that she was too afraid to admit it to him. She thought that he would make fun of her.

Then it was Beatrice's turn to be tricked. This time Hero and Ursula, a lady-in-waiting, talked about Beatrice as if Beatrice was not there. They said that Benedick was in love with Beatrice, but that he was afraid that she would laugh at him. Then they said that Beatrice was so proud that she probably couldn't love anyone. This last sentence really struck Beatrice. She too began to see Benedick differently and began to think that maybe she should love him.

Now, it seemed that maybe there would be a double wedding: Hero and Claudio, and Beatrice and Benedick. But Don John was just beginning his plot. He came in person to Claudio and told him that he had terrible news: Hero had a secret lover! He told Claudio and Don Pedro to come that night under her window and they could see for themselves. Claudio reacted very badly to this information. He said that he would disgrace Hero in the church on her wedding day if what Don John had said was true.

Before you read

1 Transform the words given to complete the gaps. Then listen and check.

Most of the people who 0........*were*........ staying at
Leonato's house went to bed early that night.

BE

They were all going to Claudio and Hero's
1......................... the next morning and they wanted to
rest.

WED

Leonato's house was 2......................... by the local
constables.

PROTECT

Dogberry was in charge of them, and his second in
command was Verges. They had decided to employ extra
men because of the 3......................... of the Prince in the
house, and the important wedding.

PRESENT

Dogberry was not a very intelligent man, but he was
honest, and he took his duties very 4......................... .

SERIOUS

He looked at the new recruits 5......................... .

CARE

'Right,' he 6........................., 'you must all listen to me.

ANNOUNCE

I'll tell you what you have to do. You walk around the
gardens at night, and if you see 7......................... strange,
you stop them. Is that clear?'

ONE

'What do we do if the person 8......................... obey us?'
one of the new constables asked.

DO

'If that happens, don't do anything,' Dogberry told the
man. 'If someone doesn't obey you, let him go.

That kind of person can be 9........................., you know!'

DANGER

'Another thing,' Dogberry went on. 'Don't make a noise
as you walk about. We don't want to disturb people.

Don't wake people up by 10......................... loudly.'

TALK

CHAPTER SEVEN

The Constables do their Duty

 ost of the people who were staying at Leonato's house went to bed early that night. They were all going to Claudio and Hero's wedding the next morning and they wanted to rest.

Leonato's house was protected at night by the local constables. Dogberry was in charge of them, and his second in command [1] was Verges. They had decided to employ extra men because of the presence of the Prince in the house, and the important wedding.

Dogberry was not a very intelligent man, but he was honest, and he took his duties very seriously. He looked at the new recruits [2] carefully.

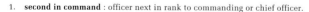

1. **second in command** : officer next in rank to commanding or chief officer.
2. **recruits** : members.

The Constables do their Duty

'Right,' he announced, 'you must all listen to me. I'll tell you what you have to do. You walk around the gardens at night, and if you see anyone strange, you stop them. Is that clear?'

'What do we do if the person doesn't obey us?' one of the new constables asked.

'If that happens, don't do anything,' Dogberry told the man. 'If someone doesn't obey you, let him go. That kind of person can be dangerous, you know!'

'Another thing,' Dogberry went on. 'Don't make a noise as you walk about. We don't want to disturb people. Don't wake people up by talking loudly.'

END

'I'd rather sleep than talk,' one of the new constables joked.

'Well said!' Dogberry told the man. 'You can't make any mistakes if you go to sleep. But remember,' he continued, 'you have to go to all the alehouses. ¹ Tell the people who have drunk too much that they should go home to bed.'

'What if they don't obey us?' someone asked again.

'Leave them alone if they don't obey you,' Dogberry advised. 'You don't want to get into arguments with people who have been drinking. And the same for thieves,' he told them. 'If you meet any thieves, stay away from them. No good can come from mixing with thieves.'

Dogberry and Verges left the new constables outside Leonato's house. They sat quietly and began talking about their new job.

'It'll be easy,' one of them said happily. 'We'll just sit quietly here for a couple of hours, and then we'll all go home to bed.'

Borachio and Conrad were also outside Leonato's house. They were talking excitedly to each other.

'I've just earned a thousand ducats!' Borachio boasted.

One of the new constables heard Borachio's voice. He made a sign to the others to be quiet.

---

1. **alehouses** : pubs.

Much Ado About Nothing

'Something's going on,' he warned them. 'I know that man, and I don't trust him. He must be up to something! [1] Let's listen, and see what happens.'

The constables sat very quietly and listened.

'A thousand crowns!' Conrad said. 'How did you earn such a lot of money?'

'It was easy,' Borachio boasted [2] again. 'I spent the evening with Hero's lady-in-waiting, Margaret,' he explained with a laugh. 'She's just leant [3] out of Hero's window to say goodnight to me. Claudio and the Prince saw everything!'

1. **up to something** : doing something suspicious.
2. **boasted** : talked with too much pride about something that you did.
3. **leant** : was in a position that was not straight.

The Constables do their Duty

'They thought Margaret was Hero?' Conrad asked.

Borachio laughed again.

'That's right. Claudio is furious with Hero – he'll never marry her now!'

The constables had heard enough. They decided to arrest Borachio and Conrad. They did not understand what the two men were doing, but they were suspicious. Suddenly they moved forward.

'You're under arrest!' one of them said loudly. 'You must come with us.'

Borachio and Conrad looked at the constables in surprise. They did not know what to do.

'Come on,' the constables said again, 'you two are coming with us. Dogberry will want to talk to you.'

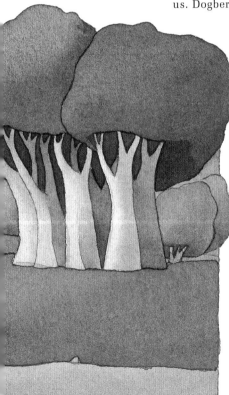

Dogberry and Verges arrived at Leonato's house very early the next morning. They were both excited and very pleased with themselves. They asked to speak to Leonato.

Leonato smiled at the two men. He was in a very good mood because of the wedding of Hero and Claudio.

'Well, my friends,' he said politely, 'what can I do for you? As you can imagine, this is a very busy day for me.'

'I'll tell you, sir,' Dogberry began.

'That's right,' Verges said hurriedly.

Much Ado About Nothing

'Please forgive my colleague, sir,' Dogberry said to Leonato. 'He is an old man, and he is a little confused in his thoughts. But he is a very honest man, all the same.'

'Very true, that's very true,' Verges agreed. 'I am an old man – but I'm an honest old man. Very true, very true – you expressed that very well!' he complimented [1] Dogberry.

Leonato was a little impatient now.

'If you have something to tell me, please say it!' he ordered.

'The constables have arrested two thieves,' Verges said.

'Correct,' Dogberry confirmed. 'The constables have arrested two thieves – and we would like to question them in front of you, sir. That's why we're here, sir.'

'Question [2] these men yourselves,' Leonato said. 'I'm too busy today. Question them, and come and tell me what you've learned from them later.'

'Yes, sir,' Dogberry said eagerly. 'We'll question them for you. We'll find out everything, I can promise you that.'

1. **complimented** : praised.
2. **question** : ask somebody questions.

Go back to the text

1 **Answer the following questions.**

   a. Who is in charge of the local constables?

   ....

   b. What was he like?

   ....

   c. Why were there extra constables?

   ....

   d. Dogberry gives some strange commands. Find some examples, and say what is strange about them.

   ....

   e. How did Borachio earn a thousand ducats?

   ....

   f. What does Dogberry request of Leonato?

   ....

   g. Does Leonato consent? Why or why not?

   ....

'He must be up to something!'

Phrasal Verbs

Go on
a. *Go on* – start to function.
   *The lights **have** just **gone on**.*
b. *Go on* (followed by a gerund) – continue an activity without a break.
   *She **went on** working. She didn't stop for lunch.*
c. *Go on* (generally used in continuous tenses) – to take place, to happen.
   *What is **going on**?*

Be up to
a. *Be up to* (followed by a gerund) – to be physically or mentally fit enough to do something.
   ***Are** you **up to** doing the exam?*
b. *Be up to* (can be used alone or it can be followed by words like *something*, *no good*, *mischief*) – to be doing something wrong.
   *What **is** that man **up to**?*
c. *Be up to you* (can be followed by an infinitive with *to*) – to be your responsibility.
   ***It's up to you** to do the shopping.*

2 **A.** The phrasal verbs *go on* and *be up to* are each used once in this chapter. Find them and then decide which of the meanings is correct for them here.

a. Go on ☐
b. Be up to ☐

B. Now complete the gaps in the following sentences with either *go on* or *be up to* to make logical affirmative or negative sentences.
Put the phrasal verbs in either the Present Simple, Present Continuous or Past Simple according to the context. The verbs in brackets have to be written either as an infinitive with 'to' or as a gerund.

Example: Benedick is sick with love.
He ..isn't up to telling.... (tell) jokes.

a. I hear somebody yelling outside. What .... out there?

b. It .... you (decide) if you want to marry her or not.

c. When I learned that Hero was dead, I .... (cry) for hours and hours.

d. I saw Don John talking quietly to his friends. I am certain that he .... something.

e. I turned the switch but the light ...., so we used candles.

f. Claudio is your friend. Are you sure that you .... (fight) him?

Who was she?

3 Use the clues to do this puzzle and find the name of a famous English writer, whose prose versions of Shakespeare's comedies became classics in their own right.

This is a prose version of *Much Ado About Nothing* especially written for students of the English language, but it is not the first prose version of this play. In fact, a brother (1775-1834) and a sister (1764-1847) prepared prose versions of Shakespeare's comedies and tragedies to introduce young readers of their day to the fabulous [1] world of Shakespeare (the sister prepared the comedies and the brother the tragedies).
They tried to use, when possible, only those words which Shakespeare himself would have used and not to use any words that had been introduced into the language after his death.

---

1.   **fabulous** : extremely good or impressive.

They tried to stress the virtuous [1] aspects of Shakespeare's plays. Their collection, later known as *Tales from Shakespeare*, was written particularly for young girls (little boys were generally allowed access to their father's library much earlier than little girls). Great care was always taken to protect the virtue of little upper-class girls.

And yet the story of this brother and sister is tragic: on 22 September 1796 the sister, during a temporary attack of insanity, [2] killed her mother with a kitchen knife. She would have spent the rest of life in an asylum for the insane, if her brother had not agreed to become her legal guardian. They spent the rest of their lives together.

Her brother became a famous writer, first for his essays on Elizabethan dramatists and then for his pleasant conversational essays in the London Magazine under the pen-name 'Elia'.

1. If you .... to do something, you are able to do it, even though it is quite difficult.
2. My brother is quite lazy. He .... ever works.
3. When you think about it, it is really terrible how Claudio decided to .... Hero in church.
4. Beatrice and Benedick are both very ...., especially when they are insulting each other.
5. If it is raining tomorrow, we will have to .... the football match.
6. I really love *Much Ado About Nothing*, but my friend can't .... it. She thinks it is boring and artificial; also she doesn't like the way the women are portrayed.
7. The opposite of ugly, used for men.
8. He .... because he was so embarrassed.

1. **virtuous** : behaving in a moral or good way.
2. **insanity** : the state of being mad.

Before you read

1 Listen to the first part of Chapter Eight and indicate who says the following sentences: *Beatrice, Don John, Leonato, Hero, Don Pedro*. Then read the chapter and say why they say them.

a. 'Claudio has come here to be married to Hero – it's you who will marry Hero, friar!'

....

....

b. 'Of course he doesn't!'

....

....

c. 'Unless you give her back to him!'

....

....

d. 'Don't give your friend a rotten gift.'

....

....

e. 'Are you well?'

....

....

f. 'I didn't speak to any man last night.'

....

....

g. 'I'm sorry for your wickedness.'

....

....

h. 'This is no place for us.'

....

....

i. 'Help her!'

....

....

CHAPTER EIGHT

A Wedding Scandal

All of Leonato's guests went to the church to see the wedding of Claudio and Hero. There was a lot of happy conversation as they waited for the priest to begin the service.

'Let's have a quick ceremony, Friar Francis,' Leonato advised.

The friar nodded [1] his head, and then he began the ceremony. First he turned to Claudio.

'Have you come here to marry Hero?' he asked.

The young man looked at the friar for a second before he answered. Then he said loudly, 'No, I have not.'

For a moment Leonato was astonished. Then he smiled.

'Quite right, quite right,' he said. 'Claudio has come here to be married to Hero – it's you who will marry Hero, friar!'

---

1. **nodded** : moved his head up and down as a sign of agreement.

The friar turned to Hero.

'Have you come here to be married to Claudio?' he asked her.

'Yes, I have,' Hero replied.

The friar looked seriously at Hero and Claudio for a moment.

'Do either of you know anything that makes you think this marriage should not take place?' he asked.

Claudio looked at Hero fiercely.

'Do you know any reason why we should not marry?' he asked her.

'No, I don't,' Hero told him.

'And you, Claudio, do you know any reason?' the friar asked.

'Of course he doesn't!' Leonato interrupted.

Claudio now turned to Leonato.

'Are you happy to give me your daughter?' he asked.

'Yes, I am,' Leonato replied.

'Must I give you something in exchange for this precious gift?' Claudio asked.

'Of course not,' Leonato said.

'Unless you give her back to him!' interrupted Don Pedro.

Claudio now raised his voice.

'Leonato, take your daughter back again,' he began. 'Don't give your friend a rotten [1] gift. Your daughter looks lovely, I admit, but she's dishonourable. I don't want her!'

1. **rotten** : not good enough to use.

A Wedding Scandal

There was a shocked silence in the church. Everyone was listening to the conversation between Claudio and Leonato.

'Speak honestly,' Leonato ordered Claudio. 'What are you trying to tell me?'

'I will never marry Hero,' Claudio replied loudly. 'She is disloyal.'

Hero blushed. She could not believe what Claudio was saying about her.

'Are you well?' she asked him faintly.

Leonato spoke to the Prince. He hoped that Don Pedro would be able to help him.

'Say something, sir,' he suggested.

'What can I say?' the Prince replied very seriously. 'I am ashamed that I encouraged Claudio to marry Hero. She is not worthy of him.' [1]

Leonato was astonished.

'I can't believe that this is happening,' he said. 'Tell me it's all a bad dream!'

'I want to ask your daughter one question,' Claudio told Leonato. 'Tell her to answer it truthfully, please.'

'I order you to answer his question truthfully,' Leonato told Hero. 'You must tell the truth.'

Claudio studied Hero's face for a moment before he spoke.

'You were speaking to a man from your window last night,' he told her. 'Who was that man?'

'I didn't speak to any man last night,' Hero answered him.

'You're lying!' Don Pedro told her angrily. 'We were outside your window last night, Claudio and I. We saw you talking to a man, Hero!' He turned to Leonato. 'It's all true, my old friend, I swear [2] it,' he said sadly. 'Your daughter has a lover.'

Don John now stepped forward. He was very pleased at the effect of his plan.

---

1. **is not worthy of him** : does not deserve him.
2. **swear** : promise.

Much Ado About Nothing

'It's no good,' he said to Hero. 'We know what kind of girl you are. I'm sorry for your wickedness!' he added.

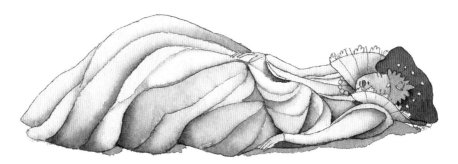

Suddenly Hero went very pale. She began to tremble, [1] and then she fell to the floor of the church. She lay on the floor without moving.

Don John looked down at her where she lay on the floor.

'Come on,' he said to the Prince and Claudio. 'This is no place for us.' He led them out of the church.

Benedick and Beatrice ran forward to help Hero.

'Help her!' Beatrice cried. 'Help her, uncle!'

'She'll be all right in a minute,' Friar Francis said gently. 'She's only fainted.'

'All right?' Leonato said angrily. 'I hope she dies, friar! Hero has brought dishonour on our family. I hope she dies,' he repeated angrily.

Friar Francis held up his hand.

'Listen to me,' he said to Leonato. 'I have been watching Hero very carefully. I believe that she is innocent. You can call me a fool if you like,' he went on, 'but I believe there has been a mistake.'

'No, friar,' Leonato said sadly. 'It's impossible, I'm afraid. You heard what Claudio and the Prince said. They both saw her talking to a man from her window – the evidence is clear!'

1. **tremble** : shake.

A Wedding Scandal

Hero now opened her eyes. She looked up at the crowd of people standing around her. The friar spoke to her gently.

'Were you speaking to a man last night?' he asked her kindly.

'No, friar,' Hero replied. 'I swear it, I'm telling the truth, friar.'

'I believe her,' Friar Francis said again. 'There has been a mistake.'

'Claudio and Don Pedro are both honest men,' Benedick said thoughtfully. 'They would never invent a story like this. But Don John,' he went on, 'he might have done it! Don John hates the Prince.'

'I will never forgive Hero if she is lying,' Leonato said, 'but I will defend her if someone is lying about her. I may be an old man,' he announced proudly, 'but I can still fight to protect my family!'

'I have an idea,' the friar said quietly. 'Claudio and the others think that Hero is dead. Let's pretend that she really is dead for a while. You, Leonato, prepare a lavish [1] funeral for her.'

'I don't understand, friar,' Leonato said. 'What's the point of pretending that Hero is dead?'

'When people hear that Hero is dead,' the friar explained, 'they will feel sorry for her. Claudio will remember that Hero died as a result of his accusation. He will wonder whether he was right about her. That will be one good result.'

Benedick liked the friar's suggestion.

'Claudio is my best friend,' he said, 'but I like this plan of yours, friar. I'll do everything I can to help you.'

'Very well,' Leonato agreed. 'We will pretend that Hero is dead.'

Friar Francis and Leonato left the church secretly with Hero. Benedick and Beatrice were alone together. Benedick looked tenderly at Beatrice.

'Have you been crying all this time?' he asked her gently.

'Yes, and I think I'm going to go on crying for a while,' Beatrice replied.

'I think Hero is innocent,' Benedick told her.

---

1. **lavish** : very expensive.

'I wish someone could prove that she's innocent,' Beatrice said.

'I have something strange to tell you,' Benedick began softly. 'I don't know how this has happened, but I love you, Beatrice.'

'How strange,' Beatrice replied. 'I feel the same. I don't know how it's happened, but I think I love you, too.'

'I'd do anything for you!' Benedick told her eagerly.

'Kill Claudio, then!' Beatrice answered.

'Kill Claudio? Never!' Benedick replied in surprise.

'Then you don't really love me,' Beatrice said sadly. 'You won't fight my enemy.'

'Why is Claudio your enemy?' Benedick asked.

'Claudio has behaved very badly,' Beatrice said angrily. 'He didn't cancel the wedding when he heard this story about Hero. No, he came to the church, and then he accused her in public – I hate him for what he has done to Hero!'

'Listen, Beatrice...' Benedick interrupted her.

'She would never talk to a man from her window,' Beatrice continued angrily. 'She loves Claudio, I know she does!'

'Do you really think that Claudio has behaved badly?' Benedick asked.

'Of course I do!'

'Then I'll fight him!' Benedick announced. 'I love you, Beatrice – I'll fight Claudio for you,' he promised.

Go back to the text

1 **Answer the following questions.**

    a. Why does the Prince feel ashamed?

    ....

    b. Why is Don Pedro so sure that Hero has a lover?

    ....

    c. How does Hero react to the accusation that she has a lover?

    ....

    d. Why is Leonato also convinced of his own daughter's guilt?

    ....

    e. Who thinks that Hero is innocent?

    ....

    f. What is Friar Francis's plan?

    ....

    g. What does Beatrice want Benedick to do to prove his love for her?

    ....

    h. Does Benedick say he will do it?

    ....

'Have you been crying all this time?'

Present Perfect Continuous

The Present Perfect Continuous tense (*have + been + present participle*) has two main uses in English.

The first use is to express the duration of an action that has not yet finished or has just finished.
*I **have been running** for two hours.*
*She **has been crying** all this time.*
*He **has been living** here for six months.*

The second use is to describe an action that has just finished. Often we can see evidence of the action.
*You look tired. What **have you been doing**?*
*I **have been typing** letters all morning.*

89

If we wish to talk about the result of the action, we use the Present Perfect.

*How many letters **have you typed?***

***I've typed** about twenty.* (result, the number of letters produced)

*You smell of onions. **Have you been cooking?***

*Yes, I **have been cooking**.*

***I have cooked** dinner for thirty people.* (result, a dinner for thirty people)

*Your hands are covered in oil. What **have you been doing?***

***I have been repairing** your bike.*

***I have repaired** your bike.* (result, you can now ride it)

2 **Put the verbs in brackets into the Present Perfect or Present Perfect Continuous according to the context.**

Example: Benedick's hands are stained with ink. (He/write love poems).
           He's been writing love poems................

a. (I/write some poems for you). There they are on the table.
    ....

b. (John/read *Much Ado About Nothing* and *The Tempest*). He is not finished,
    but he is very tired.
    ....

c. (John/read *Much Ado About Nothing* and *The Tempest*). He's now ready to
    take the English literature examination.
    ....

d. (The constables/interrogating Borachio for an hour).
    ....

e. Look at the smile on Don Pedro's face! (Balthazar/sing Don Pedro's favourite
    song).
    ....

f. (Benedick/be in Messina for a week already).
    ....

g. (Beatrice and Benedick/arguing again). Look how red in the face they are!
    ....

h. (I/sit by Hero's tomb since last night).
    ....

i. (The cook/bake cakes). That's why there is flour all over the floor.
    ....

j. (The cook/bake some cakes). Would you like one?
    ....

FCE

3 Benedick is now very confused and very happy and very different! He had always said that he would never fall in love, but now everything has changed.

Imagine that you are Benedick and write a letter to your friend Ferdinand in Padua to explain the changes in your life.

In your letter you wish to answer the following questions.

1. Who is Beatrice and how has she changed your life?
2. Who is Claudio and how has Hero changed his life?

You should begin your letter like this. Write between 120 and 180 words.

Dear Ferdinand,

Here in Messina there has been much ado about nothing! Everybody is going crazy, including me! Do you remember how I used to say that .... Well now I am different.

....

....

....

....

....

....

....

....

....

....

....

Your loyal friend,
Benedick

Women in Shakespeare's Comedies

The theatre in Shakespeare's day was treated with great suspicion by the authorities. Plays were regarded as an immoral form of entertainment, and the authorities made sure that theatres were built far away from city centres.

The morality of the time made it difficult for dramatists to create convincing parts for female characters. There were two main reasons for this. Firstly, there was a convention [1] that women could not appear on stage, so boys or men had to perform female roles. Secondly, audiences expected the action to focus on male heroes or villains.

In his comedies Shakespeare plays with these stage conventions with great success. In *As You Like It*, for example, a female character (played by a male actor) pretends to be a boy in love with another female character (played by a male actor). A similarly complicated situation occurs in *Twelfth Night*. The twins Sebastian and Viola are separated after a shipwreck. Viola (played by a male actor) disguises herself as a boy, and finds work as a servant to Duke Orsino. Viola falls in love with the duke, but cannot declare her love because she is supposed to be a boy. The duke is in love with Olivia, but she falls in love with Viola, whom she believes to be a boy. The situation is complicated even further when Sebastian arrives on the scene.

Shakespeare also uses his genius to portray strong, independent and intelligent women. Much of the interest in *The Taming of the Shrew*, for example, derives from the intensity and wit of Katharine's conversations with Petruchio. The same is true in *Much Ado About Nothing*, and the jokes and insults between Benedick and Beatrice. One recurrent [2] theme in the comedies is the conflict between men and women, and the resolution of this conflict through love and marriage. In *The Taming of the Shrew*, for example, Katharine's

Ellen Terry as Beatrice and Henry Irving as Benedick, 1882.

1. **convention** : a traditional way of doing something.
2. **recurrent** : happening repeatedly.

anger and aggression [1] mean that she is rejected by the men of her society. It is the outsider, Petruchio, who proves himself even more aggressive than she is, and leads her to acknowledge [2] the importance of love. In *A Midsummer Night's Dream* there is conflict between the King and Queen of the fairies, Oberon and Titania. As in *The Taming of the Shrew*, harmony can only be restored when Titania submits to [3] her husband.

The theme of conflict between men and women is also present in *Much Ado About Nothing*. The play opens with the arrival of Don Pedro, Claudio and Benedick from a successful military campaign. As soon as they arrive Benedick and Beatrice continue their own private war – a conflict based on irony and insults.

At the beginning of the play Benedick and Beatrice compete against each other, and seem to have a genuine dislike of each other. Their mutual [4] dislike is really based on mutual attraction. This is indicated very early in the play, before Don Pedro's plan is put into action. Benedick compares Beatrice and Hero. He says that Beatrice is more beautiful than Hero, in the same way that 'the first of May' is more beautiful than 'the last of December'.

David Garrick as
Benedick, 1748.

1 **Answer the following questions.**

    a. Why were theatres built outside the centre of London?
    ....

    b. Who played the female parts in Shakespeare's plays?
    ....

    c. How did Shakespeare use the conventions regarding female actors to his advantage?
    ....

---

1. **aggression** : angry feelings or behaviour that often result in fighting.
2. **acknowledge** : admit that something is true.
3. **submits to** : accepts somebody's power or control.
4. **mutual** : felt or done by two people towards each other.

d. What kind of female characters did Shakespeare create?

....

e. How is the war between men and women resolved in Shakespeare's plays?

....

f. What kind of 'war' do Benedick and Beatrice fight?

....

g. What is the real source of the apparent dislike between Beatrice and Benedick?

....

Before you read

1 **Listen to the first part of Chapter Nine and then complete the sentences.**

a. Claudio does not wish to fight Leonato because Leonato ....

....

b. Although he believes that Hero is dead, the Prince is still convinced that she was ....

c. At first, Claudio is happy to see Benedick because he hopes that Benedick will

....

d. Benedick comes to ask Claudio ....
but the Prince thinks that Benedick came to joke with his friend.

e. Benedick will .... if Claudio refuses to fight him.

f. Dogberry has discovered that Borachio and Conrad ....

....

g. Borachio tells Don Pedro that Don John ....

CHAPTER NINE

Dogberry and his Men discover the Truth

eonato was very angry and disturbed by what had happened in the church. His brother, Antonio, tried to calm him, but it was no good.

'Don't tell me to be calm!' the old man cried. 'I love Hero, and I can't bear the idea that she has been dishonoured. I can't bear it, I tell you!' he shouted.

'Don't make yourself suffer,' Antonio advised him. 'Think of the people who accused her. It's only right that they should suffer, too.'

'You're right,' Leonato agreed. 'I'm sure that Hero is innocent. Claudio and the Prince have lied about her.'

Suddenly, the Prince and Claudio appeared. They were embarrassed to see Leonato and his brother after what had happened. They bowed awkwardly [1] and began to walk away.

---

1. **awkwardly** : in a way that shows one's embarrassment.

'Just a moment,' Leonato called after them. 'I want to speak to you. You have wronged my daughter.'

'Don't quarrel with us,' Don Pedro advised him.

'You, Claudio, you have behaved badly,' Leonato shouted. 'You lied about Hero, and now she's dead. I'm going to fight you, young man!'

'You're too old for fighting,' Claudio replied. 'I won't fight you, Leonato.'

Antonio stepped forward angrily.

'Then you'll fight me, young man,' he announced. 'I'm not too old for fighting. I loved my niece. You'll fight me, I say!' he repeated.

Now Leonato was worried. His brother did not know that Hero was still alive.

'I can't let him fight Claudio,' Leonato thought. 'I must stop him.'

'Brother...' he began.

'Leave me alone!' Antonio said roughly. 'I'm not scared of fighting him. I know what these young men are like!'

'But, Antonio.' Leonato said desperately.

'Leave me alone, I say!' Antonio said to Leonato. 'Let me deal with [1] this.'

'Don't quarrel, gentlemen,' the Prince said again. 'I am sorry that Hero's dead,' he told Leonato. 'But she was guilty, my friend. She was guilty.'

Leonato held onto his brother's arm.

'Come on,' he ordered him. 'We'll make them listen to us another time.'

Leonato and Antonio walked away.

Don Pedro and Claudio stood talking together. They were glad that they had avoided a fight with Leonato and Antonio. Then they saw Benedick approaching.

'Just the man we want to see,' Claudio told him happily. 'We're both sad, Benedick. We need you to cheer us up a little.'

1. **deal with** : take control of.

Dogberry and his Men discover the Truth

Don Pedro looked closely at Benedick. He noticed that the young man was very pale.

'What's the matter?' he asked.

Benedick ignored the Prince, and spoke quietly to Claudio.

'I'm going to fight you,' he whispered fiercely. 'You choose the weapons, and you choose the time. But if you don't fight me, I'll tell everyone you're a coward!'

Don Pedro did not hear what Benedick said to Claudio. He thought the two young men were having a joke together. He decided to tease [1] Benedick a little about Beatrice.

'It's really true that Beatrice loves you,' he said pleasantly. 'You'll be a married man soon, my friend – just as I told you!' he predicted with a laugh.

Benedick did not smile at the Prince's joke.

'My lord,' he said politely, 'you have always treated me well. I thank you for that. I will not serve you any longer. Your brother Don John has left Messina. The three of you have killed an innocent young child.'

Benedick walked away from Don Pedro and Claudio. He was very angry with them.

'He's serious,' Don Pedro said in surprise. He thought for a moment. 'My brother's left Messina – I wonder why!'

Just then Dogberry and some of his men came into sight. They had Borachio and Conrad with them.

'Isn't that Borachio and Conrad?' Don Pedro said to Claudio. 'I wonder why they're prisoners?' he called out to Dogberry. 'Stop! Tell me why these two men are prisoners. What have they done?'

Dogberry bowed to the Prince and Claudio.

'These two men,' he told them, 'are liars. They have told lies about a lady here in Messina, and they are bad men.'

Don Pedro now spoke to Borachio.

---

1. **tease** : make fun of.

'What have you done?' he asked.

Borachio looked ashamed.

'This constable here has found out the truth,' he said, pointing to Dogberry. 'He heard me telling Conrad about Don John's plan to deceive you and Claudio. It was your brother who invented the story about Hero. It was Margaret you saw in Hero's clothes talking to me. Hero was innocent. And now she's dead. I am very sorry, sir.'

'Poor Hero!' Claudio groaned. 'I should have believed in you.'

He began to weep. [1]

'Leonato knows everything by now,' Dogberry said to the Prince. 'We sent him a message as soon as we discovered the truth. But here he is,' he said, 'I see him coming now.'

'Where's the man who killed my daughter with his lies?' Leonato shouted loudly.

Borachio looked ashamed.

'It was me, sir,' he said humbly. 'I killed your daughter.'

'You didn't do it by yourself,' Leonato told him angrily. 'Don John, Don Pedro and Claudio are also responsible for death.'

'You're right, Leonato,' Claudio said quietly. 'I was wrong, I treated Hero badly. You must punish me if you wish. But I made an honest mistake.'

'Me, too,' Don Pedro said sadly. 'I made an honest mistake, but you have suffered, Leonato. I wish I could do something to help you.'

'You can't bring my daughter back,' Leonato said sternly. 'But there is something you can both do for Hero. Tell the people of Messina that my daughter was innocent. And tonight, go to her grave and pray for her there. Write an epitaph [2] for her tomb. Will you do that for Hero?'

---

1. **weep** : cry.
2. **epitaph** : poem in praise of a dead person.

Don Pedro and Claudio agreed to go to Hero's grave that night.

'And you, Claudio,' Leonato went on, 'there's something else you can do. My brother Antonio has a daughter. She's very like poor Hero. Marry my brother's daughter, just as you would have married mine. Will you do that?'

Claudio bowed his head.

'I'll marry your niece,' he said. 'It's the least I can do to make peace between us again.'

'Then come to my house tomorrow morning,' Leonato ordered. 'In the meanwhile, I want to speak to Margaret – I don't believe she knew anything about Don John's wicked plan.'

'She didn't, sir!' Borachio said. 'Margaret's a good girl – she knew nothing about it!'

Meanwhile Benedick had decided to write Beatrice a poem. He was not a good poet, however, and writing was difficult. The first line of the poem came easily:

'The god of love,'

'That's good,' he thought, 'very direct and very romantic. Now what shall I put?' He thought for a moment, and then he wrote:

'The you of love,
That sits above.'

'This is easy!' he told himself. He thought again.

'The god of love,
That sits above,
And knows me, and knows me,
How much I deserve...'

Much Ado About Nothing

Benedick threw the pen down onto the table in disgust. He could not think of anything else to say. He went for a walk in Leonato's garden. Here he met Beatrice, and the two lovers began talking.

'I've spoken to Claudio,' Benedick told her. 'He knows he has to fight me, or I will tell everybody that he's a coward. But tell me,' he asked, 'what made you fall in love with me?'

'All your bad qualities,' Beatrice joked. 'There are a lot of them, you know. And what about you,' she asked, 'what made you love me?'

'I never meant to love you,' Benedick told her simply. 'And how is Hero?' he asked seriously.

'She's very unhappy,' Beatrice told him.

Suddenly, they heard someone running towards them. It was Ursula, one of Hero's ladies-in-waiting. She called loudly to Beatrice.

'You must come quickly, Beatrice,' Ursula said. 'Everything's going to be all right. Hero's innocent – it was all a plot by Don John to hurt the Prince and Claudio. Come quickly!'

Benedick and Beatrice smiled at each other. This was good news indeed.

'Let's go and hear this news together,' Beatrice suggested.

'Let's,' agreed Benedick. He held out his hand, and Beatrice took it. They walked quickly towards the house.

Go back to the text

1 Indicate whether the following statements are true (T) or false (F), and then correct the false ones.

	T	F
a. Leonato does not want Antonio to fight Claudio because Antonio does not know that Hero is still alive.	☐	☐
b. Leonato is not really convinced of Hero's innocence.	☐	☐
c. Benedick does not want to serve Don Pedro because Don Pedro is Don John's brother.	☐	☐
d. Dogberry knows that Borachio and Conrad were involved in a plan to destroy Hero's reputation.	☐	☐
e. Margaret also waits to ruin Hero's reputation.	☐	☐
f. Even after Borachio's confession, Don Pedro still feels responsible for Hero's death.	☐	☐
g. Claudio agrees to marry Hero's niece.	☐	☐
h. Benedick is a very good poet.	☐	☐

'We'll make them listen to us another time.'

Make and let

Look at the sentences below.

All have the same structure, *verb + object + infinitive* (without to).

Make can mean either force or cause.
*We **made them listen** to us.* = We forced them to listen to us.
*Wine **makes me feel** sleepy.* – Wine causes me to feel sleepy.

Let means allow.
*Leonato **let** Antonio deal with the problem.* = Leonato allowed Antonio to deal with the problem.
Let can be used in a few common expressions with different meanings.
***Let** me know* = Communicate to me that information.
***Let** me go* = Release me.
***Let** me in* = Open the door so I can come in.
***Let** me out* = Open the door so I can get out.

2 Make logical sentences using either *make* or *let*. Put the verb in the tense indicated in brackets.

Example: All of Benedick's bad qualities/Beatrice fall in love with him.
(Past Simple)
All of Benedick's bad qualities made Beatrice fall in love with him.

a. Don Pedro and Claudio/Benedick think that Beatrice was in love with him. (Past Simple)

....

b. Before Benedick met Beatrice, he/not/any woman love him.
(Past Perfect)

....

c. Don John's hatred of his brother/not/him live in peace.
(Present Simple)

....

d. Leonato/Claudio marry Hero.
(Future going-to)

....

e. As we can see in this play love/people do strange things.
(Present Simple)

....

f. Antonio/not/his brother fight Claudio.
(Future going-to)

....

g. Dogberry/drunks go home. He never arrests them.
(Present Simple)

....

h. Leonato/not/Don John escape.
(Past Simple)

....

i. Leonato/not/Claudio know that Hero was really alive.
(Present Perfect)

....

And Keanu Reeves plays the part of Don John!

---------- **FCE** ----------

3 You want to get the video of Kenneth Branagh's film version of *Much Ado About Nothing*. Your friend, however, thinks that a film based on a play by Shakespeare will be really, really boring. Write a letter using the following information to convince your friend that she will really enjoy it. Write between 120 and 180 words.

The Critic's name	Their rating	What they said
James Berardinelli	5	For those who don't find Shakespeare's comedies funny, this is the film to see, because it's hilarious. [1]
Roger Egbert	5	Branagh is nothing if not a film director of high spirits and great energy.
Leonard Maltin	5	The film is rowdy, [2] high spirited and remarkably fast paced.

Some of the famous actors in the film, and the roles they play	Other films they have acted in
Kenneth Branagh, Benedick	Henry V
Emma Thompson, Beatrice	The Remains of the Day, In the Name of the Father
Denzel Washington, Don Pedro	Philadelphia, Malcolm X, A Soldier's Story
Keanu Reeves, Don John	Speed, Johnny Mnemonic
Michael Keaton, Dogberry	Beetle Juice, Batman

Other facts you might want to use to convince your friend.

* Kenneth Branagh is also the director of the film. He also directed *Henry V*, which was a great success with the general public.
* Kenneth Branagh and Emma Thompson were married when the film was made, so their lovers' quarrels seem even more realistic and funny.
* This film was beautifully filmed in the splendid Tuscan countryside.
* Shakespeare was a popular entertainer, and certainly not a boring intellectual writer.

1. **hilarious** : very funny.
2. **rowdy** : noisy and uncontrolled.

You can begin like this:

Dear ....,
I know you think that Shakespeare is boring. But I've got the
film of Much Ado About Nothing because ....
....
....
....
....
....
....
....
....
....
....

Before you read

FCE

1 Listen to the first part of Chapter Ten and say whether the following sentences
are true (T) or false (F). Then read the text and correct the false ones.

		T	F
a.	Don Pedro has composed an epitaph for Hero.	☐	☐
b.	Don Pedro and Claudio stay in the church next to Hero's tomb all night.	☐	☐
c.	Leonato still thinks that Don Pedro and Claudio are guilty of hurting his daughter.	☐	☐
d.	Claudio is going to marry Antonio's daughter.	☐	☐
e.	Now, Benedick does not want to marry Beatrice.	☐	☐
f.	At first Claudio does not recognise Hero because she is wearing a mask.	☐	☐

CHAPTER TEN

Two Weddings

hat night Claudio and Don Pedro went back to the church, as they had promised Leonato. Claudio had composed an epitaph for Hero. He read from the poem as he walked along:

> *Hero was killed by slanderous* [1] *tongues*
> *And here she lies*
> *Death rewards her awful wrongs*
> *By giving her fame that never dies.*
> *The life that died with shame*
> *Lives on in glorious fame.*

Don Pedro and Claudio stayed near the tomb all night, praying and talking about Hero. They were both very sad. At last the inside of the church began to glow with light – it was morning.

'Come on, Claudio,' Don Pedro said, 'it's time to go to Leonato's house.'

---

1. **slanderous** : false.

Much Ado About Nothing

Remember you are going to marry Antonio's daughter this morning – you promised you would.'

Claudio stood up. He was tired after the long night in the church.

'I'm ready,' he said quietly. 'I hope this wedding will be happier than the last one!' He looked sadly towards Hero's tomb as he spoke.

There was great excitement in Leonato's house that morning. The friar, in particular, was very happy.

'I told you Hero was innocent!' he kept saying to Leonato. 'Didn't I say she was innocent, all the time?'

Leonato smiled at the friar.

'And Claudio and Don Pedro are innocent, as well,' he said. 'It was all Don John's fault – and the Prince will surely see that he is punished for what he did. Margaret was innocent, as well,' he went on. 'It's true that Borachio was her lover – but she did not know anything about the wicked plot against Hero.'

'I'm glad that everything's worked out ¹ well,' Antonio said.

'Me, too,' Benedick said. 'I thought I was going to have to fight my best friend Claudio.'

'Now, Antonio,' Leonato said, 'you know what we're going to do when Claudio and Don Pedro arrive. Claudio has promised to marry your daughter. We will pretend that Hero is your daughter. She will wear a heavy mask. Claudio will be marrying the girl he loves, but he won't know it – it'll be a great joke!' he cried with a happy laugh.

'I must say something, sir,' Benedick told Leonato. 'I'm in love with your niece, Beatrice, and she's in love with me – I want your permission to marry her.'

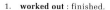

1. **worked out** : finished.

Two Weddings

'Just as Don Pedro and Claudio predicted!' Leonato said with a smile. 'I give you my permission to marry Beatrice.'

'And I will perform the ceremony!' the friar offered excitedly.

It was not long before Don Pedro and Claudio arrived at Leonato's house. They exchanged polite greetings with everyone.

'Well, Claudio,' Leonato said sternly, 'do you remember your promise? Are you ready to marry Antonio's daughter?'

'I'll keep my promise,' Claudio said seriously.

'Go and call her,' Leonato ordered Antonio.

Antonio came back into the room a few minutes later with Beatrice, Hero, Margaret and Ursula all wearing masks – it was impossible to see their faces.

'Which one am I going to marry?' Claudio asked nervously.

Antonio pointed to Hero.

END

Claudio stepped forward.

'We are going to be husband and wife,' he said gently. 'May I see your face before the wedding?'

'No!' Leonato cried. 'You may not see her face until the wedding is concluded.'

'Then take my hand,' Claudio said. 'I will lead you to the friar. I will be your husband if you wish it.'

He put out his hand. Hero put out her own hand, and grasped [1] his.

'I've been your wife before,' she said quietly. She removed her mask.

Claudio looked into her face. He gasped, and the tears came into his eyes.

'Another Hero!' he whispered in astonishment.

'The first Hero died in shame,' Hero said quietly, 'and here I am, another one.'

'It really is Hero!' Don Pedro cried. 'She didn't die at all!'

Claudio stood in silence. He could not speak for happiness. The friar touched his arm.

'I'll explain everything,' he said softly. 'But first, let's have the wedding!'

Now Benedick stepped forward.

'One moment, Friar Francis,' he said softly. 'Which one is Beatrice?'

Another girl in a mask came forward.

'I am,' she answered quietly. 'What do you want, Benedick?'

'Do you love me?' Benedick asked her.

'Beyond reason, [2] no,' she replied with a smile.

'Then Don Pedro, Claudio and Leonato were wrong,' Benedick said. 'They told me you loved me madly.' [3]

'And you,' Beatrice asked. 'Do you love me, Benedick?'

'Beyond reason, no,' he answered with a smile.

1. **grasped** : held tightly.
2. **beyond reason** : not reasonable or acceptable.
3. **madly** : passionately.

'Then Margaret, Ursula and Hero were wrong,' Beatrice told him. 'They said you loved me madly.'

'They told me you were sick for love of me,' Benedick said.

'They told me you were nearly dead for love of me,' Beatrice replied.

'Then you really don't love me?' Benedick asked her.

'Not really,' Beatrice admitted. 'I only love you because you love me.'

'This is all nonsense!' Claudio said loudly. 'Benedick loves Beatrice, I'm sure of it. Look, I've got a poem he wrote to her!' Claudio showed the others Benedick's poem.

Now Hero spoke as well.

'And Beatrice loves Benedick!' she said loudly. 'I've got a letter she wrote to him. Look, here it is!' She showed everyone Beatrice's letter to Benedick.

Benedick laughed.

'We do not love each other,' he joked, 'but it seems our hands are in love. Let's marry, all the same.'

Beatrice laughed as well.

'I'll marry you,' she joked, 'but only to save your life, Benedick – they said you were so unhappy without me!'

Go back to the text

1 **Choose the best answers (a, b, c or d) for the following questions.**

1. Who had always believed that Hero was truly innocent?
   - a. Don Pedro.
   - b. Leonato.
   - c. The friar.
   - d. Claudio.

2. Why was Benedick going to fight Claudio?
   - a. Because Claudio had insulted Beatrice.
   - b. Because Beatrice had insulted Claudio.
   - c. Because Leonato would not let him marry Beatrice if he did not fight for his daughter's good reputation that had been ruined by Claudio.
   - d. Because Beatrice told him to do it.

3. What did Claudio promise Leonato that he would do?
   - a. Marry Hero's cousin.
   - b. Fight Benedick.
   - c. Leave Messina immediately and never return.
   - d. Fight Don John.

4. Why didn't Claudio recognise Hero until after the wedding was concluded?
   - a. Because she was facing the other way.
   - b. Because her face had changed so much because of her great suffering.
   - c. Because she was wearing a mask.
   - d. Because Claudio's eyes were so full of tears he could not see well.

5. Why did Claudio show everybody the love poem that Benedick had written for Beatrice?
   - a. Because he wanted everybody to see that Benedick was a terrible poet.
   - b. Because he wanted to tease his friend.
   - c. Because Benedick refused to admit that he was in love with Beatrice, and the poem was proof that he really did love her.
   - d. Because Claudio was tired of hearing Benedick and Beatrice argue all the time, and he wanted them to admit that they loved each other.

FCE

2 **Below is a summary of Chapters 7-10, but four paragraphs (a, b, c and d) have been left out. Put them in the right place in the summary. Then complete the gaps in the passage with the correct words from the text.**

a. At this point, the happy love story almost becomes a tragedy. Leonato and Benedick both wanted to fight Claudio. Fortunately, at this point Dogberry told Claudio and Don Pedro that Hero was [1]........................ . Claudio began to weep because he thought that his accusations had really killed Hero. Then Leonato appeared. He admitted that Claudio and Don Pedro had made an honest [2]........................ but he wanted Claudio to do something to make up for his behaviour. Claudio had to tell all of Messina that Hero was innocent, he had to write an [3]........................ for her tomb and spend the whole night in the church praying. Finally, he wanted Claudio to marry Hero's [4]........................ .

b. The next day the two [1]........................, Dogberry and Verges, brought Borachio and Conrad to Leonato. Dogberry explained that he had captured these two thieves and wanted to [2]........................ them in front of Leonato. However, Leonato was too busy thinking about his daughter's [3]........................ and did not want to be bothered. He told the constables to interrogate them by themselves.

c. Now it was Benedick's turn to get married. The friar called Beatrice. Benedick asked her if she loved him, but she would not say that she did. At this point, Benedick wouldn't admit that he loved Beatrice. Both of them were too proud. Fortunately, Claudio and Hero intervened. Claudio had a [1]........................ Benedick had written for Beatrice and Hero had a love [2]........................ that Beatrice had written to Benedick. So, it was clear that they loved each other and should marry. Benedick joked that [3]........................ they did not love each other, it seemed that their [4]........................ were in love.

d. Then the Prince and Claudio left the church. At first Leonato was very angry with Hero because he believed that she had brought [1]........................ on his family. The friar, however, did not believe that she was [2]........................ . When Hero gained consciousness again, the friar asked her if she had a lover, and Hero swore that she didn't. The friar then had an idea. He said that they should [3]........................ that Hero was dead, and that Leonato should prepare a lavish [4]........................ for her. In this way, Claudio would feel sorry for having killed her with his horrible accusations.

Dogberry was in charge of protecting Leonato's house. He was not very intelligent but he took his job 1........................ . He gave his men all sorts of absurd advice, but in the end two of them actually captured two wrong-doers: Borachio and Conrad. They had heard Borachio boasting that he had 2........................ a thousand ducats by spending the evening with Hero's 3........................ Margaret. The Prince and Claudio had seen Margaret when she leant out the window to say goodnight to Borachio, and they thought that she was Hero!

That day the wedding took place. The friar began the service, but Claudio interrupted him. He told Leonato that his daughter was a 1........................, and that he was sure that she was disloyal to him. Then both Claudio and Don Pedro swore that Hero had a secret lover. Then the man behind the 2........................, Don John intervened. He told Hero that he was sorry for her 3........................, but that she could not hide the facts. Hero started to 4........................ and then she fell to the floor.

Everyone then left the church except Beatrice and Benedick. When they looked at each other, they made a strange discovery: they loved 1........................! Benedick even said that he would do anything for Beatrice. Beatrice told him they he had to fight Claudio because he was now her 2........................ . At first Benedick refused, but then he accepted to fight his best 3........................ .

So, Claudio spent the night by Hero's 1........................ . The next day, as he had promised, he went to the church to marry whom he thought was Hero's cousin. Benedick also wished to be married that same day to Beatrice and he asked Leonato for permission. Leonato gladly agreed it. Hero wore a 2........................ so Claudio did not recognise her. After the ceremony Hero removed her mask. When he saw her he 3........................ and 4........................ came to his eyes.

A lot of bother¹ about love

1 Find out how the word *ado* is used in modern English and then write a short composition to explain why you think Shakespeare gave the title *Much Ado About Nothing* to this play. Write between 120 and 180 words.

2 *Much Ado About Nothing*, a tragedy or a comedy?
As you have read, this comedy has a lot in common with the tragedy *Romeo and Juliet*. In *Romeo and Juliet* the tragic chain of events begins when a letter arrives late. How would you change *Much Ado About Nothing* to make it a tragedy? How would the story end? Write a composition of between 120 and 180 words.

Lines from Shakespeare

1 Read the extracts from Shakespeare's original play. For each dialogue explain briefly what is happening.

2 Find lines in the dialogues which mean:

a. Do not arrest any vagabond. Let him go and be thankful that a bad person has gone away.

b. I will marry you only because I feel sorry for you.

c. While she is writing on sheets of paper she imagines Benedick and herself between the sheets of a bed.

d. I will marry you because otherwise you will die of a terrible disease.

e. If you should some day fall in love you will be a very interesting subject of conversation.

f. On the outside she seems honourable because she is so lovely, but inside she is really a terrible person.

ACT ONE SCENE 1

a) BEATRICE: Who is his companion now? He hath every month a new sworn brother.
MESSENGER: Is't possible?
BEATRICE: Very easily possible. He wears his faith but as the fashion of his hat, it ever changes with the next block.
MESSENGER: I see, lady, the gentleman is not in your books.
BEATRICE: No. An he were, I would burn my study.

1.   **bother** : trouble or difficulty.

ACT ONE SCENE 1

[b] DON PEDRO: I shall see thee, ere I die, look pale with love.

BENEDICK: With anger, with sickness, or with hunger, my lord; not with love. Prove that ever I lose more blood with love than I will get again with drinking, pick out mine eyes with a ballad-maker's pen and hang me up at the door of a brothel house for the sign of blind Cupid.

DON PEDRO: Well, if ever thou dost fall from this faith, thou wilt prove a notable argument.

ACT TWO SCENE 1

[c] BEATRICE: Lord, I could not endure a husband with a beard on his face. I had rather lie in the woollen.

LEONATO: You may light on a husband that hath no beard.

BEATRICE: What should I do with him – dress him in my apparel and make him my waiting-gentlewoman? He that hath a beard is more than a youth, and he that hath no beard is less than a man; and he that is more than a youth is not for me; and he that is less than a man, I am not for him.

ACT TWO SCENE 3

[d] DON PEDRO: Hath she made her affection known to Benedick?

LEONATO: No, and swears she never will. That's her torment.

CLAUDIO: 'Tis true, indeed, so your daughter says. 'Shall I,' says she, 'that have so oft encountered him with scorn, write to him that I love him?'

LEONATO: This says she now when she is beginning to write to him, for she'll be up twenty times a night, and there will she sit in her smock till she have writ a sheet of paper. My daughter tells us all.

CLAUDIO: Now you talk of a sheet of paper, I remember a pretty jest your daughter told us of.

LEONATO: O, when she had writ it and was reading it over, she found Benedick and Beatrice between the sheet?

CLAUDIO: That.

ACT TWO SCENE 3

[e] BENEDICK: They say the lady is fair. 'Tis a truth, I can bear them witness. And virtuous – 'tis so, I cannot reprove it. And wise, but for loving me. By my troth, it is no addition to her wit – nor no great argument of her folly, for I will be horribly in love with her.

ACT THREE SCENE 3

(f) DOGBERRY: This is your charge: you shall comprehend all vagrom men.
You are to bid any man stand, in the Prince's name.

WATCHMAN: How if a will not stand?

DOGBERRY: Why then take no note of him, but let him go, and presently
call the rest of the watch together, and thank God you are rid of a
knave.

VERGES: If he will not stand when he is bidden, he is none of the Prince's
subjects.

DOGBERRY: True, and they are to meddle with none but the Prince's
subjects. You shall also make no noise in the streets, for the watch to
babble and to talk is most tolerable and not to be endured.

SECOND WATCHMAN: We will rather sleep than talk. We know what
belongs to a watch.

ACT FOUR SCENE 1

(g) FRIAR: If either of you know any inward impediment why you should not
be conjoined, I charge you on your souls to utter it.

CLAUDIO: Know you any, Hero?

HERO: None, my lord.

FRIAR: Know you any, Count?

LEONATO: I dare make his answer – none.

CLAUDIO: O, what men dare do! What men may do! What men daily do,
not knowing what they do!

BENEDICK: How now! Interjections? Why then, some be of laughing, as 'ah!
ha! he!'

CLAUDIO: Stand thee by, friar. Father, by your leave,
Will you with free and unconstrainèd soul
Give me this maid, your daughter?

LEONATO: As freely, son, as God did give her me.

CLAUDIO: And what have I to give you back whose worth
May counterpoise this rich and precious gift?

DON PEDRO: Nothing, unless you render her again.

CLAUDIO: Sweet prince, you learn me noble thankfulness.
There, Leonato, take her back again.
Give not this rotten orange to your friend.
She's but the sign and semblance of her honour.

ACT FIVE SCENE 4

(h) BENEDICK: Do not you love me?

BEATRICE: Why no, no more than reason.

BENEDICK: Why then, your uncle and the prince and Claudio

Have been deceived. They swore you did.

BEATRICE: Do not you love me?

BENEDICK: Troth no, no more than reason.

BEATRICE: Why then, my cousin, Margaret, and Ursula.

Are much deceived, for they did swear you did.

BENEDICK: They swore that you were almost sick for me.

BEATRICE: They swore that you were well nigh dead for me.

BENEDICK: 'Tis no such matter. Then you do not love me?

BEATRICE: No, truly, but in friendly recompense.

LEONATO: Come, cousin, I am sure you love the gentleman.

CLAUDIO: And I'll be sworn upon't that he lovers her,

For here's a paper written in his hand,

A halting sonnet of his own pure brain,

Fashioned to Beatrice.

HERO: And here's another,

Writ in my cousin's hand, stol'n from her pocket,

Containing her affection unto Benedick.

BENEDICK: A miracle! Here's our own hands against our hearts. Come, I

will have thee, but by this light, I take thee for pity.

BEATRICE: I would not deny you, but by this good day, I yield upon great

persuasion, and partly to save your life, for I was told you were in a

consumption.

Much Ado About Nothing

Playscript

Act ✛ One

A street in Messina. LEONATO, HERO and BEATRICE are walking together.
Enter a MESSENGER.

MESSENGER: The Prince of Aragon is coming to Messina. He will arrive soon.

LEONATO: I see that Don Pedro is very pleased with Claudio.

BEATRICE: What about Benedick? Have you got any news about him?

MESSENGER: He, too, has come home safely. He is famous for his humour.

BEATRICE: His humour's the only good thing about him.

MESSENGER: Benedick is not in your good books.

BEATRICE: If Benedick were in my good books, I would never read them again.

Enter DON PEDRO, DON JOHN, BENEDICK and CLAUDIO.

LEONATO: Welcome to Messina. I am happy that you will be my guest while you are here.

DON PEDRO: Is this beautiful young girl your daughter?

LEONATO: Yes. At least her mother has always said Hero was my daughter!

BENEDICK: Do you doubt it, sir?

BEATRICE: What a fool you are. Can't you see how everyone is laughing at you?

BENEDICK: I see you're still alive, Lady Scornful.

BEATRICE: Of course I'm still alive. My scorn feeds off you – didn't you know that?

BENEDICK. All the ladies love me, except you. But I don't care for any of them.

BEATRICE: At least you won't marry one of them and make her unhappy.

Everyone moves towards Leonato's house, except CLAUDIO and
BENEDICK.

CLAUDIO: I want to talk to you. Did you notice Leonato's daughter Hero? Did you see how beautiful she is?

BENEDICK: You're in love! But surely you're not thinking of getting married?

CLAUDIO: If Hero would marry me, I'd certainly be very happy!

DON PEDRO re-enters.

DON PEDRO: What are you two talking about? Is it a secret?

BENEDICK: Claudio is in love with Hero – that's our secret, sir!

DON PEDRO: You'll fall in love one day, my young friend. I shall see you pale with love one day.

BENEDICK: Never! I'll never surrender to just one woman.

Act ⁑ Two

The garden in Leonato's house. Enter DON PEDRO and CLAUDIO.

DON PEDRO: What's all this about you and Hero?

CLAUDIO: I liked her when I saw her last, before we went away to the war. Now that I've seen her again, I'm sure of it – that's the girl for me!

DON PEDRO: She's a beautiful girl, and she comes from a good family. I'll do what I can to help you. There's going to be a big party at Leonato's house tonight. Everybody will be wearing masks. I'll talk to Hero. I'll pretend to be you, you see?

Enter one of Antonio's servants. He hides behind a tree, to hear what DON PEDRO and CLAUDIO are saying.

CLAUDIO: What do you mean, sir?

DON PEDRO: I'll tell Hero I love her. I'll tell her I can't live without her. Then I'll go to her father and tell him everything.

SERVANT: Don Pedro's in love with Hero – I must go and tell my master immediately!

Exit the servant.

DON PEDRO: Then you'll be able to marry her!

LEONATO and ANTONIO meet in the house.

ANTONIO: I've got some extraordinary news for you!

LEONATO: What kind of news?

ANTONIO: The Prince is in love with your Hero. One of my servants saw Don Pedro and Claudio talking together. The Prince said he would speak to Hero at the party tonight. He's going to tell her he loves her!

LEONATO: I'd better tell Hero about this – then she'll know what to do if the Prince speaks to her.

A room in Leonato's house. DON JOHN, CONRAD and BORACHIO are talking together.

DON JOHN: What's the news, Borachio?

BORACHIO: Claudio is going to marry Hero.

DON JOHN: Claudio – I hate that young man! I wish I could do something that would damage Claudio. Will you two help me?

BORACHIO: Whatever you wish, sir – you know that.

CONRAD: I'll do what I can to please you, sir.

Act ⁜ Three

The masked ball at Leonato's house. Enter HERO, DON PEDRO, CLAUDIO, BENEDICK, wearing masks.

DON PEDRO: Will you walk with me?

HERO: I'll walk with you if you are handsome, and if you don't talk too much.

DON PEDRO: Let's talk about love.

Another part of the chamber.

BENEDICK: Someone told me that you get all of your jokes from books.

BEATRICE: I bet it was Benedick who said that. He doesn't like me at all – it's just the kind of thing Benedick would say about me!

BENEDICK: Who's Benedick?

BEATRICE: Oh, he's Don Pedro's clown. He's a fool really, and not funny at all. He just says rude things about everyone, and that makes fools laugh. If people don't laugh at what he says, he gets very unhappy. He thinks he's very clever, but everyone hates him, really.

Another part of the chamber.

DON JOHN: You're Benedick, aren't you? You're a friend of my brother the Prince. Please tell him that he cannot marry Hero. She does not come from a noble family.

CLAUDIO: What makes you think Don Pedro wants to marry Hero?

DON JOHN: I heard them talking. He told her he loves her. I don't like it at all!

Exit DON JOHN. Enter BENEDICK.

BENEDICK: You've heard the news? The Prince has stolen Hero from you, Claudio!
CLAUDIO: Leave me alone, Benedick, just leave me alone!

Act ✧ Four

BENEDICK and DON PEDRO talking outside the chamber.

DON PEDRO: Have you seen Claudio? I want to talk to him.
BENEDICK: He's in the hall. He's very upset. You shouldn't have stolen Hero from him.
DON PEDRO: I haven't stolen Hero from Claudio. I've just asked Leonato if Claudio can marry her! By the way, why is Beatrice so angry with you?
BENEDICK: It's a silly business – I can't stand her!

Enter CLAUDIO and HERO, holding hands and smiling. BEATRICE enters with them.

DON PEDRO: You see, I told you the truth. Leonato has said that Claudio and Hero can be married. Now do you believe that I'm Claudio's friend?
BEATRICE: Everyone is getting married except me.
DON PEDRO: I'll find you a husband.
BEATRICE: Thank you, sir, but I'll never marry.

Exit BEATRICE. DON PEDRO, LEONATO and CLAUDIO remain talking together.

DON PEDRO: Well, you'll be a married man one week from now.
CLAUDIO: I wish the wedding were tomorrow!
DON PEDRO: I know you're impatient, but we'll make this week a very pleasant one for you. I'm going to arrange another wedding – between Beatrice and Benedick! Will you all help me to arrange it?
LEONATO: Very well.
CLAUDIO: Of course we will.
HERO: I promise.
DON PEDRO: I've got a plan.

Another room in the house. DON JOHN, BORACHIO and CONRAD are talking together.

BORACHIO: I think I know how we can spoil this wedding.

DON JOHN: Well, what is it? What are we going to do?

BORACHIO: You know that I'm very close to Margaret – very, very close, if you know what I mean?

DON JOHN: How can that help us?

BORACHIO: Don Pedro thinks that Hero is a beautiful and honourable girl. Go and tell him that she is not honourable at all, sir. Tell the Prince that Hero has a secret lover – me! Say that you can prove it. Make Claudio and Don Pedro stand under Hero's bedroom window. I will then stand at the window. I'll talk to Margaret as if she were Hero. The Prince and Claudio will think Hero is in love with me – Claudio will call off the wedding!

DON JOHN: It might just work! Let's try your plan, Borachio.

Act ✦ Five

The garden. BENEDICK is walking by himself, when he sees DON PEDRO, CLAUDIO, LEONATO and OTHERS. He hides in order to hear what they are saying.

DON PEDRO: What was that you were saying before, about Beatrice being in love with Benedick?

LEONATO: It's true. She loves him, there's no doubt about that.

DON PEDRO: What makes you think she's really in love?

LEONATO: She told you all about it, didn't she?

CLAUDIO: She's really in love. She told me herself. But she can't tell him, you see, because she thinks Benedick would just laugh at her.

LEONATO: She's even tried writing a letter to tell him what she feels. But she didn't send it. Poor girl, she's suffering very badly!

DON PEDRO: Let's help Beatrice by letting Benedick know that she loves him.

CLAUDIO: No, no! Benedick would just laugh at her. We mustn't say anything, sir.

Exit DON PEDRO, LEONATO and CLAUDIO. BENEDICK remains alone in the garden.

BENEDICK: They say she loves me. Perhaps I've been wrong about her. She's a lovely girl, after all!

BEATRICE comes into the garden.

BEATRICE: I've been sent to look for you. Dinner is ready, and everyone is waiting for you.

BENEDICK: Thank you for the trouble you have taken to find me.

BEATRICE: Trouble? It was no trouble to come and look for you.

BENEDICK: If it was no trouble, perhaps it was a pleasure to come and look for me?

BEATRICE: What makes you think it was a pleasure?

BEATRICE walks back to the house. BENEDICK watches her thoughtfully.

BENEDICK: There's no doubt about it. She said it was 'no trouble' to come and look for me. She really does love me!

Later in the garden. HERO and URSULA are talking. BEATRICE is listening to their conversation.

HERO: Poor Benedick is terribly in love with Beatrice.

URSULA: Are you sure? I thought that Benedick did not like Beatrice at all.

HERO: Claudio and the Prince told me all about it. They asked me to talk to Beatrice, but I said it would do no good. Beatrice is very proud, and she would just laugh at Benedick.

URSULA: You're probably right. Beatrice is so proud that she can't love anyone. It's better not to say anything to her about Benedick. She would just make the poor man suffer horribly with her cruelty and her jokes.

HERO: I'm going to talk to Benedick. I'm going to tell him that he's far too good for Beatrice.

URSULA: It's true that Benedick is very handsome.

HERO and URSULA leave the garden. BEATRICE is left alone.

BEATRICE: My friends think I am too proud! They say Benedick is a good man. Perhaps they're right – perhaps I should love Benedick!

Act ✤ Six

Enter DON PEDRO, LEONATO, CLAUDIO and BENEDICK.

DON PEDRO: I must go home after your wedding.

CLAUDIO: Then I will accompany you. It's the least I can do after your kindness to me.

DON PEDRO: No. You don't want to go on a long journey just after your wedding. No, I'll take Benedick with me. The journey will be short once he starts telling his jokes and stories.

BENEDICK: I'm not as witty as I once was. I don't know why it is.

CLAUDIO: You do look quite sad. Is anything the matter?

BENEDICK: It's just a toothache.

DON PEDRO: I never knew that toothache could make a man look sad, Benedick.

CLAUDIO: I think he's in love. Look at the careful way he's dressed, and the trouble he takes with his hair – he's a man in love, I tell you!

BENEDICK frowns angrily at his friends' jokes, then he touches LEONATO's arm and goes away with him. DON PEDRO and CLAUDIO are left alone.

DON PEDRO: He's going to speak to Leonato! He's going to ask for permission to marry Beatrice.

Enter DON JOHN. He greets DON PEDRO and CLAUDIO politely.

DON JOHN: I have something to tell you.

DON PEDRO: Is it something private, or can Claudio stay and hear?

DON JOHN: My news is about Hero. I've discovered that she is not an honourable girl – she has a lover! I can prove that Hero is disloyal to you. Come with me tonight, both of you. We'll stand outside Hero's bedroom window – you'll see that what I've told you is the truth!

CLAUDIO: I can't believe it!

DON PEDRO: Neither can I!

DON JOHN: I don't want you to make a terrible mistake, Claudio. You can't marry a girl who behaves like Hero – she would dishonour you!'

CLAUDIO: Very well, I'll come with you tonight. If you're right about Hero I'll disgrace her at the church tomorrow morning. I'll tell everyone what sort of girl she is!

Act + Seven

Messina at night. Enter DOGBERRY and other constables.

DOGBERRY: I'll tell you what you have to do. You walk around the gardens at night, and if you see anyone strange, you stop them. Is that clear?

WATCHMAN: What do we do if the person doesn't obey us?

DOGBERRY: If someone doesn't obey you, let him go. That kind of person can be dangerous, you know! Don't make a noise as you walk about. We don't want to disturb people. Don't wake people up by talking loudly.

WATCHMAN: I'd rather sleep than talk.

DOGBERRY: Well said! You can't make any mistakes if you go to sleep. But remember, you have to go to all the alehouses. Tell the people who have drunk too much that they should go home to bed.

WATCHMAN: What if they don't obey us?

DOGBERRY: Leave them alone if they don't obey you. You don't want to get into arguments with people who have been drinking. And the same thing for thieves. If you meet any thieves, stay away from them. No good can come from mixing with thieves.

Exit DOGBERRY. Enter BORACHIO and CONRAD.

BORACHIO: I've just earned a thousand crowns!

WATCHMAN: Ssh! I know that man, and I don't trust him. Let's listen, and see what happens.

CONRAD: A thousand crowns! How did you earn such a lot of money?

BORACHIO: It was easy. I spent the evening with Hero's lady-in-waiting, Margaret. She's just leant out of Hero's window to say goodnight to me. Claudio and the Prince saw everything!

CONRAD: They thought Margaret was Hero?

BORACHIO: That's right. Claudio is furious with Hero – he'll never marry her now!

WATCHMAN: You're under arrest! Come on, you're coming with us. Dogberry will want to talk to you.

A room in Leonato's house, very early the next morning. DOGBERRY, VERGES and LEONATO are talking.

LEONATO: Well, my friends, what can I do for you?

DOGBERRY: I'll tell you, sir.

VERGES: The constables have arrested two thieves.

DOGBERRY: Correct, the constables have arrested two thieves. We want to question them in front of you, sir. That's why we're here.

LEONATO: I'm too busy today. Question them, and come and tell me what you've learned from them later.

Act ❖ Eight

The church. All the main characters are present.

FRIAR FRANCIS: Have you come here to marry Hero?

CLAUDIO: No, I have not.

LEONATO: Quite right, quite right. Claudio has come here to be married to Hero – it's you who will marry Hero, friar!

FRIAR FRANCIS: Do either of you know anything that makes you think this marriage should not take place? Do you, Claudio?

LEONATO: Of course he doesn't!

CLAUDIO: Are you happy to give me your daughter?

LEONATO: Yes, I am.

CLAUDIO: Must I give you something in exchange for this precious gift?

LEONATO: Of course not.

DON PEDRO: Unless you give her back to him!

CLAUDIO: Take your daughter back again. Don't give your friend a rotten gift. Your daughter looks lovely, I admit, but she's dishonourable. I don't want her! She is disloyal.

DON PEDRO: I am ashamed that I encouraged Claudio to marry Hero. She is not worthy of him.

LEONATO: I can't believe that this is happening.

CLAUDIO: I want to ask your daughter one question. You were speaking to a man from your window last night. Who was he?

HERO: I didn't speak to any man last night

DON PEDRO: You're lying! We saw you talking to a man, Hero!

HERO faints, and falls to the floor of the church. DON PEDRO and CLAUDIO walk out of the church.

BEATRICE: Help her! Help her, uncle!

LEONATO: I hope she dies! Hero has brought dishonour on our family.

FRIAR FRANCIS: I have been watching Hero very carefully. I believe that she is innocent. I believe there has been a mistake.

LEONATO: It's impossible. Claudio and the Prince both saw her talking to a man. The evidence is clear!

HERO regains consciousness.

FRIAR FRANCIS: Were you speaking to a man last night?

HERO: No, I swear it.

FRIAR FRANCIS: I believe her. There has been a mistake somewhere. I have an idea. Claudio and the others think that Hero is dead. Let's pretend that she really is dead for a while.

LEONATO: What's the point of pretending that Hero is dead?

FRIAR FRANCIS: When people hear that Hero is dead, they will feel sorry for her. Claudio will remember that Hero died as a result of his accusation. He will wonder whether he was right about her.

BENEDICK: I like this plan of yours, friar. I'll do everything I can to help you.

Everyone leaves the church except BENEDICK and BEATRICE.

BENEDICK: I think Hero is innocent.

BEATRICE: I wish someone could prove that she's innocent.

BENEDICK: I have something to tell you. I love you, Beatrice.

BEATRICE: How strange, I feel the same. I don't know how it's happened, but I think I love you, too.

BENEDICK: I'd do anything for you!

BEATRICE: Kill Claudio, then!

BENEDICK: Kill Claudio? Never!

BEATRICE: Then you don't really love me. You won't fight my enemy.

BENEDICK: Why is Claudio your enemy?

BEATRICE: Claudio has behaved very badly. I hate him for what he has done to Hero!

BENEDICK: Listen, Beatrice…

BEATRICE: She would never talk to a man from her window. She loves Claudio, I know she does!

BENEDICK: Do you really think that Claudio has behaved badly?

BEATRICE: Of course I do!

BENEDICK: Then I'll fight him! I'll fight Claudio for you.

Act ✦ Nine

LEONATO and ANTONIO in a street in Messina.

LEONATO: Don't tell me to be calm! I love Hero, and I can't bear the idea that she has
  been dishonoured.
ANTONIO: Think of the people who accused her. It's only right that they should suffer.
LEONATO: You're right. I'm sure that Hero is innocent. Claudio and the Prince have
  lied about her.

  Enter DON PEDRO and CLAUDIO.

LEONATO: Just a moment. I want to speak to you. You have wronged my daughter.
  Claudio, you lied about Hero, and now she's dead. I'm going to fight you, young man!
CLAUDIO: You're too old for fighting. I won't fight you, Leonato.
ANTONIO: Then you'll fight me, young man. I loved my niece. You'll fight me, I say!
LEONATO: Brother…
ANTONIO: Leave me alone! I'm not scared of fighting him.
DON PEDRO: Don't quarrel, gentlemen. I am sorry that Hero's dead, but she was guilty.

  LEONATO leads ANTONIO away. DON PEDRO and CLAUDIO remain talking.
  Enter BENEDICK.

CLAUDIO: You're just the man we want. We're both sad, Benedick. We need you to
  cheer us up a little.
BENEDICK: I'm going to fight you. If you don't fight me, I'll tell everyone you're a
  coward!
DON PEDRO: Beatrice loves you. You'll be married soon, my friend – just as I told you!
BENEDICK: My lord, you have always treated me well. I thank you for that. I will not
  serve you any longer. Your brother Don John has left Messina. The three of you
  have killed an innocent young child.

  Exit BENEDICK.

DON PEDRO: I wonder what's the matter with him!

  Enter DOGBERRY, with BORACHIO and CONRAD as prisoners.

DON PEDRO: Stop! Tell me why these two men are prisoners. What have they done?
DOGBERRY: These two men have told lies about a lady here in Messina.
BORACHIO: The constables heard me telling Conrad about Don John's plan to deceive

you and Claudio. It was your brother who invented the story about Hero. She was innocent. And now she's dead. I am very sorry, sir.

CLAUDIO: Poor Hero!

Enter LEONATO.

LEONATO: Where's the man who killed my daughter with his lies?

BORACHIO: It was me, sir.

LEONATO: You didn't do it by yourself. Don John, Don Pedro and Claudio – they killed her as well.

CLAUDIO: I was wrong, I treated Hero badly. You must punish me if you wish. But I made an honest mistake.

LEONATO: You can't bring my daughter back. Tell the people of Messina that my daughter was innocent. And tonight, come to her grave and pray for her there. Write an epitaph for her tomb. There's something else you can do. My brother Antonio has a daughter. She's very like poor Hero. Marry my brother's daughter, just as you would have married mine. Will you do that?

CLAUDIO: I'll marry your niece. It's the least I can do.

Act ⁑ Ten

A church at night. DON PEDRO and CLAUDIO are praying.

DON PEDRO: It's time to go. Remember you are going to marry Antonio's daughter this morning – you promised you would.

CLAUDIO: I'm ready.

Leonato's house that morning.

FRIAR FRANCIS: I told you Hero was innocent! Didn't I say she was innocent, all the time?

LEONATO: Claudio and Don Pedro are innocent, as well. It was all Don John's fault. Now, Antonio, you know what we're going to do when Claudio and Don Pedro arrive. We will pretend that Hero is your daughter. She will wear a heavy mask. Claudio will be marrying the girl he loves, but he won't know it – it'll be a great joke!

BENEDICK: I'm in love with your niece, Beatrice – I want your permission to marry her.

LEONATO: Just as Don Pedro and Claudio predicted! I give you my permission to marry Beatrice.

Enter DON PEDRO and CLAUDIO.

LEONATO: Well, Claudio, do you remember your promise? Are you ready to marry Antonio's daughter?

CLAUDIO: I'll keep my promise.

ANTONIO leaves the room. He returns with HERO and BEATRICE, who are wearing masks.

CLAUDIO: We are going to be husband and wife. May I see your face before the wedding?

LEONATO: No! You may not see her face until the wedding is concluded.

CLAUDIO: Then take my hand. I will lead you to the friar. I will be your husband if you wish it.

HERO: I've been your wife before.

HERO removes her mask.

CLAUDIO: Another Hero!

HERO: The first Hero died in shame. Here I am, another one.

DON PEDRO: It really is Hero – she didn't die at all!

FRIAR FRANCIS: I'll explain everything. But first, let's have the wedding!

BENEDICK: One moment, Friar Francis. Which one is Beatrice?

BEATRICE: I am. What do you want, Benedick?

BENEDICK: Do you love me?

BEATRICE: Beyond reason, no.

BENEDICK: Then Don Pedro, Claudio and Leonato were wrong. They told me you loved me madly.

BEATRICE: And you, do you love me, Benedick?

BENEDICK: Beyond reason, no.

BEATRICE: Then Margaret, Ursula and Hero were wrong. They said you loved me madly.

BENEDICK: Then you really don't love me?

BEATRICE: Not really. I only love you because you love me.

CLAUDIO: This is all nonsense! Benedick loves Beatrice, I'm sure of it. Look, I've got a poem he wrote to her!

HERO: And Beatrice loves Benedick! I've got a letter she wrote to him. Look, here it is!

BENEDICK: We do not love each other, but it seems our hands are in love. Let's marry, all the same.

BEATRICE: I'll marry you, but only to save your life, Benedick – they said you were so unhappy without me!

EXIT TEST

Focus on the context

1 Answer the following questions.

   a. Where and when was William Shakespeare born?

   b. In which language did Shakespeare study at the local grammar school?

   c. How many plays did Shakespeare write?

   d. When was *Much Ado About Nothing* written?

   e. What type of play is it?

SCORE /5

Focus on the story

E **2** For questions 1-12, choose the correct answers (A, B, C or D).

   1. What was the messenger's reaction to Beatrice's comments about Benedick?

      A He was amused.

      B He was furious.

      C He was embarrassed.

      D He was unhappy.

   2. What does Leonato joke about with Benedick?

      A The fact that Benedick constantly changes friends.

      B The fact that Hero cannot possibly be Benedick's daughter.

      C The fact that Benedick is famous for his humour.

      D The fact that Beatrice was rude about Benedick.

3. What did Antonio's servant understand?

    ☐ **A** That Claudio was in love with Hero.

    ☐ **B** That Don John was in love with Hero.

    ☐ **C** That Benedick was in love with Hero.

    ☐ **D** That Don Pedro was in love with Hero.

4. What type of daughter is Hero?

    ☐ **A** A dutiful one.

    ☐ **B** A disobedient one.

    ☐ **C** An arrogant one.

    ☐ **D** A defiant one.

5. What was Borachio's plan?

    ☐ **A** To help arrange a wedding between Beatrice and Benedick.

    ☐ **B** To help spoil the wedding between Claudio and Hero.

    ☐ **C** To help arrange a wedding between Margaret and Claudio.

    ☐ **D** To help Don Pedro fall in love with Beatrice.

6. How are both Beatrice and Benedick tricked?

    ☐ **A** They are both asked to listen to each other declaring their love.

    ☐ **B** Claudio talks to Benedick and Hero talks to Beatrice.

    ☐ **C** Balthazar plays them both a song to show them that they love each other.

    ☐ **D** They both overhear conversations in the garden which claim that they are in love with each other.

7. What terrible news did Don John bring?

    ☐ **A** That Claudio was in love with someone else.

    ☐ **B** That Leonato had just decided that Hero couldn't marry Claudio after all.

    ☐ **C** That Hero was in love with someone else.

    ☐ **D** That Hero had just had a terrible accident.

8. How much money did Borachio earn?

- [ ] **A** A hundred ducats.
- [ ] **B** Five hundred ducats.
- [ ] **C** A thousand ducats.
- [ ] **D** A hundred thousand ducats.

9. What happened at the church in front of the friar?

- [ ] **A** Beatrice and Benedick decided to get married.
- [ ] **B** Hero married Don Pedro instead of Claudio.
- [ ] **C** Beatrice fainted because she was accused of having a secret lover.
- [ ] **D** Claudio announced in public that he didn't want to marry Hero any more.

10. Whose lies killed Leonato's daughter?

- [ ] **A** Borachio's.
- [ ] **B** Claudio's.
- [ ] **C** Dogberry's.
- [ ] **D** Conrad's.

11. What was Claudio's reaction when he realised he was really marrying Hero?

- [ ] **A** Horrified, as he still felt she was guilty.
- [ ] **B** Upset, because he liked the idea of marrying Hero's cousin.
- [ ] **C** Overjoyed, because he really loved Hero.
- [ ] **D** Shocked, because he wasn't sure he loved her any more.

12. Who did Benedick finally marry?

- [ ] **A** Hero.
- [ ] **B** Margaret.
- [ ] **C** Ursula.
- [ ] **D** Beatrice.

SCORE /12

3 Are the following questions true (T) or false (F)? Correct the false sentences.

		T	F
a.	Leonato, the Governor of Messina, had two daughters, Hero and Beatrice.	☐	☐
b.	Beatrice was always very polite about Benedick.	☐	☐
c.	Claudio fell in love with Hero and lost all interest in the army.	☐	☐
d.	Don Pedro came up with a good idea to let Hero know that Claudio was in love with her.	☐	☐
e.	Don John hated Claudio.	☐	☐
f.	Hero always refused to do what her father told her to.	☐	☐
g.	At the party at Leonato's house, Beatrice spoke to Don Pedro.	☐	☐
h.	Benedick overheard Leonato, Claudio and Don Pedro saying that Beatrice was in love with him.	☐	☐
i.	Beatrice wasn't meant to overhear Hero talking to Ursula and Margaret about herself.	☐	☐
j.	Benedick said he looked sad because he had a headache.	☐	☐
k.	Don John told Leonato and Claudio that Hero wasn't an honourable girl.	☐	☐
l.	Hero died on the day of her wedding to Claudio.	☐	☐
m.	Beatrice believed that Hero was innocent.	☐	☐
n.	Benedick agreed to fight Claudio because he was in love with Beatrice.	☐	☐
o.	Claudio agreed to marry Beatrice.	☐	☐
p.	Two couples finally got married.	☐	☐

SCORE ⬭ /16

TOTAL SCORE ⬭ /33

Much Ado About Nothing

KEY TO THE ACTIVITIES

Shakespeare's Life

Page 10 – exercise 1

a. He was born in Stratford-on-Avon.
CERTAIN

b. He was born on 23 April, 1564.
LIKELY

c. John Shakespeare and Mary Arden
were his parents. CERTAIN

d. He went to a local grammar school.
LIKELY

e. He was eighteen years old. CERTAIN

f. He had three children: Susanna,
Hamnet and Judith. CERTAIN

g. He was a schoolmaster. LIKELY

h. An actor in the Queen's Company
died shortly before the company
visited Stratford-on-Avon, and
Shakespeare took his place. LIKELY

i. He worked with the Lord
Chamberlain's Men which later
changed its name to the King's
Men. CERTAIN

j. His theatrical works were
published after his death. CERTAIN

Shakespeare's *Much Ado About Nothing*

Page 12 – exercise 1

a. The Prince of Aragon and Don
Pedro.

b. Benedick and Claudio.

c. Hero.

d. Beatrice.

e. Claudio.

f. The Prince and Claudio.

g. Benedick.

h. Hero.

i. Don John.

j. The local constables, Dogberry and
Verges.

Page 13 – exercise 1

1 both / **2** each / **3** at / **4** for / **5** When /
6 his / **7** the / **8** it / **9** asked / **10** is /
11 will / **12** many / **13** few / **14** killed /
15 is / **16** has / **17** about / **18** to /
19 did / **20** how

Chapter One

Page 22 – exercise 1

a. Leonato is the Governor of
Messina.

b. His daughter Hero, and his niece
Beatrice.

c. He brings a letter which says that
the Prince of Aragon is arriving
and that he has won a great
victory.

137

d. He knows that Beatrice and Benedick are always telling jokes about each other.

e. A young Florentine who is Benedick's new friend in the army.

f. One of Don Pedro's young officers.

g. His is famous for his wit and humour.

h. She jokes about him.

i. She means that he changes friends easily and often.

j. Hero.

Page 22 – exercise 2

a. At least her mother has always said Hero is my daughter! (p. 19)

b. You may see me pale with illness, or pale with anger, my Lord – but you'll never see me pale with love. (p. 21)

c. Why should I doubt it? You were still a child! (p. 19)

d. Lucky men! At least you won't make one of them unhappy. (p. 20)

e. My scorn feeds off you. (p. 20)

f. A friendship is like a hat to Benedick – it lasts until there is a new fashion! (p. 19)

Page 23 – exercise 3

a. each other	**b.** each other
c. themselves	**d.** themselves
e. each other	**f.** themselves
g. each other	

Page 23 – exercise 1

1 c. / 2 b. / 3 b. / 4 a. / 5 c. / 6 b. / 7 a. / 8 b. / 9 c. / 10 a. / 11 b.

Chapter Two

Page 29 – exercise 1

a. T

b. T

c. T

d. F – Leonato is going to have the party.

e. T

f. F – He himself is going to pretend to be Claudio.

g. F – He only wishes to help his friend.

h. T

i. F – He is very jealous of Claudio because Claudio is his brother's favourite.

Page 30 – exercise 2

a. Although Beatrice is a funny, beautiful, young woman, Benedick doesn't like her.
Beatrice is a funny, beautiful, young woman. However, Benedick doesn't like her.

b. Although I much prefer Hero, Beatrice is certainly a splendid young woman.
Beatrice is certainly a splendid young woman. However, I much prefer Hero.

c. Although Beatrice says that a friend is like a hat for Benedick, Benedick is a good and faithful friend.
Beatrice says that a friend is like a hat for Benedick. However, Benedick is a good and faithful friend.

d. Although Claudio has always said that he doesn't want to get married, he is going to marry Hero.
Claudio has always said that he doesn't want to get married. However, he is going to marry Hero.

e. Benedick will fall in love with someday, although he says that he will never surrender to one woman.
Benedick says that he will never surrender to one woman. However,

he will fall in love with someday.

f. It is really Claudio who is in love with Hero, although Antonio thinks that the Prince is in love with Hero. Antonio thinks that the Prince is in love with Hero. However, it is really Claudio who is in love with Hero.

g. Although I am Don Pedro's brother, he prefers Claudio to me. I am Don Pedro's brother. However, he prefers Claudio to me.

h. Although Don John has plotted against his brother before, they are friends now. Don John has plotted against his brother before. However, they are friends now.

Page 31 – exercise 3

1 now / **2** he loves her very much and wants to marry her / **3** says that he will pretend to be Claudio and tell her of Claudio's love / **4** hears part of what the Prince says / **5** that the Prince is in love with Hero / **6** tell / **7** the Prince's brother / **8** the Prince prefers Claudio to him / **9** plot against Claudio

Page 31 – exercise 1

a. 'A man **without** a **beard** is too young for me.' (Beatrice)

b. 'I'll **walk** with you if you are **handsome** and if you don't talk too much.' (Hero)

c. 'I want to **talk** about love.' (Don Pedro)

d. 'Benedick? **Who's** Benedick?' (Benedick)

e. 'He thinks he's very **clever**, but everyone **hates** him, really.' (Beatrice)

f. 'I don't like the **news** – I don't like it at **all**.' (Don John)

g. 'So the Prince has **tricked** me.' (Claudio)

h. 'What a **horrible** girl she is – I hate her.' (Benedick)

Chapter Three

Page 38 – exercise 1

a. I hope you will do what your father wants.

b. She will always obey her father.

c. You are lucky that I don't like you because I have a lot of bad qualities.

d. Since you are not really witty at all you have to get all of your jokes from books.

e. Everyone hates him really, although he thinks he's very clever.

f. Her family is not noble.

Page 39 – exercise 2

1. h. Shakespeare is the famous poet who wrote *Much Ado About Nothing*.

2. f. The messenger gave Leonato a letter that said that the Prince of Aragon, Don Pedro, was coming for a visit.

3. c. Don Pedro has a plan which will help Claudio win Hero.

4. g. Everybody wore masks at the party Leonato gave at his house.

5. d. Benedick is the man Beatrice likes to make fun of.

6. a. Don John has a plan that will ruin Claudio.

7. e. Beatrice is a young woman who is always making jokes.

8. b. Hero is the young woman Claudio wants to marry.

Page 40 – exercise 3

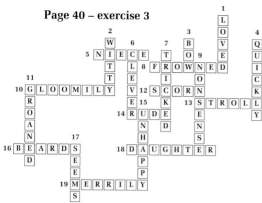

b. False – Benedick can't stand Beatrice.
c. T
d. F – He leaves because he doesn't want to talk to Beatrice.
e. T
f. F – He is being serious.
g. F – The Prince has a plan to arrange a wedding between Beatrice and Benedick.

Page 41 – exercise 4

1 c. / 5 b. / 4 e. / 3 f. / 6 a. / 2. d.

Tragic and Comic Elements in _Much Ado About Nothing_

Page 43 – exercise 1

a. Both plays are about the problems of love. They both have a helpful friar, and the heroines of the two plays, Juliet and Hero, both pretend to be dead.
b. The staged death of Juliet leads to tragedy when Romeo discovers her, but in _Much Ado About Nothing_, the staged death of Hero leads to reconciliation between her and Claudio.
c. It ends in tragedy.
d. He is a typically English comic character in the tradition of Bottom of _A Midsummer Night's Dream_.
e. It shows us how love can be created and ruined by very trivial forces.
f. He is saying that their actions come from true love even if they are not aware that they love each other.

Page 44 – exercise 1

a. T

Chapter Four

Page 50 – exercise 1

1. a. / 2. b. / 3. d. / 4. e. / 5. f. / 6. g. / 7. h. / 8. i.

Page 51 – exercise 2

a. Beatrice shouldn't have been so rude to Benedick.
b. Benedick shouldn't have tried to trick Beatrice at the party.
c. Don Pedro should have talked more quietly to Hero.
d. Claudio should have trusted Hero.
e. Nobody should have trusted Don John.
f. Benedick shouldn't have doubted that Don Pedro was really Claudio's friend.

Page 51 – exercise 3

A. 1. Present perfect
  2. Conditional
  3. Future going-to
  4. Present simple
  5. Past simple
  6. Present perfect
  7. Present simple
  8. Present simple
B. 1. Future going-to
  2. Present simple
  3. Present perfect
  4. Present simple
  5. Past simple
  6. Conditional

7. Present perfect
8. Present simple

Page 52 – exercise 4

A.
1. didn't he?
2. wasn't there?
3. did he?
4. won't you?
5. was there?
6. will you?
7. don't they?
8. haven't they?

B.
1. wasn't he?
2. didn't he?
3. aren't I?
4. wasn't he?
5. does he?
6. would she?
7. did she?
8. isn't it?

Page 53 – exercise 1

1. to / **2.** much / **3.** over / **4.** ✓ / **5.** had /
6. not / **7.** ✓ / **8.** all / **9.** myself /
10. being / **11.** ✓ / **12.** the / **13.** ✓ /
14. ✓ / **15.** to

Chapter Five
Page 61 – exercise 1

1. b. / **2. a.** / **3. a.** / **4. b.** / **5. a.** / **6. b.**

Page 62 – exercise 2

A.
1. d. Beatrice's jokes about Benedick were so rude that the messenger was shocked.
2. f. Claudio is so timid that he asked Don Pedro to talk to Hero.
3. a. Don Pedro has made such a good plan that Benedick actually believes that Beatrice loves him.
4. c. Benedick tells such funny stories that everybody always laughs.
5. e. Don John is so jealous that he has decided/decides to ruin Claudio's wedding.
6. g. Balthazar sang such a beautiful song that everyone applauded.
7. b. Claudio will be so angry when he discovers that Hero has a secret lover that he will call off the wedding.

Page 63 – exercise 3

b. *Much Ado About Nothing*, which takes place in Messina, talks about the fragility of love.
c. Beatrice, who is Hero's cousin, is always making witty remarks.
d. Don John, who is Don Pedro's brother, plots to destroy the love between Claudio and Hero.
e. Claudio, who is a brave and capable soldier, is afraid to declare his love to Hero.
f. Because of Don Pedro's clever plan Benedick, who has always sworn that he would never fall in love, is beginning to look at Beatrice differently.

Page 64 – exercise 1

1 day / **2** wedding / **3** journey / **4** place /
5 want / **6** short / **7** jokes / **8** don't /
9 exchanged / **10** serious / **11** anything /
12 make / **13** hair / **14** right / **15** explain

Chapter Six
Page 69 – exercise 1

1. a. / **2. d.** / **3. c.** / **4. a.** / **5. c.** / **6. b.**

Page 70 – exercise 2

a. distrust
b. disobedient
c. non-fiction
d. dislikes
e. unaware
f. disbelieved
g. dishonoured
h. disloyal

Page 71 – exercise 3

1. d. / **2. a.** / **3. b.** / **4. c.**

Page 73 – exercise 1

1 wedding / **2** protected / **3** presence / **4** seriously / **5** carefully / **6** announced / **7** anyone / **8** doesn't / **9** dangerous / **10** talking

Chapter Seven

Page 79 – exercise 1

a. Dogberry.
b. He was a very serious but silly man.
c. Because of the wedding in the Governor's house.
d. If someone doesn't obey you, let him go. If you meet any thieves, stay away from them. No good can come from mixing with thieves.
e. He spent the evening with Hero's lady-in-waiting.
f. He would like to question the prisoners in front of Leonato.
g. No, he doesn't. He is too busy with the wedding.

Page 80 – exercise 2

A. a. Something's going on, page 76 – Definition c.
   b. He must be up to something, page 76 – Definition b.
B. a. What's going on out there?
   b. It's up to you to decide if you want to worry her or not.
   c. I went on crying for hours and hours.
   d. I am certain the he was up to something.
   e. I turned the switch but the light didn't go on, so we used candles.
   f. Are you sure that you are up to fighting him?

Page 80 – exercise 3

The name of the famous writer is *Mary Lamb*.

1. M A N A G E
2. H A R D L Y
3. D I S G R A C E
4. F U N N Y
5. C A L L O F F
6. S T A N D
7. H A N D S O M E
8. B L U S H E D

Page 82 – exercise 1

a. Leonato says this because he does not yet understand that Claudio no longer wishes to marry Hero and that Claudio was serious when he said that he hasn't come to marry Hero.
b. Leonato says this because he believes that Claudio has no reason not to marry Hero; he still does not understand what is going on.
c. Don Pedro says this because he too believes that Hero has a lover and that Claudio very well might want to give her back.
d. Claudio says this because, indeed, he now believes that Hero is a 'rotten gift', even if she appears to be very lovely.
e. Hero says this to Claudio because she can't believe that he would say such a thing if he were not ill.
f. Hero says this to Claudio after he has accused her of being with another man.
g. Don John says this to Hero after she has tried to defend herself against their accusations.
h. Don John says this to Claudio to convince him of Hero's guilt. He believes they should leave the church.
i. Beatrice says this when Hero faints.

Chapter Eight

Page 89 – exercise 1

a. Because he encouraged Claudio to marry Hero, and she is not worthy of him.

b. Because he believes that he saw her at the window talking to her lover.

c. She is totally unbelieving. She thinks that Claudio must be ill to say such things.

d. Because he believes what Don Pedro and Claudio have said.

e. The friar.

f. He will have Claudio and Don Pedro believe that she has died.

g. Fight Claudio.

h. Yes, he does.

Page 90 – exercise 2

a. I have written some poems for you.

b. John has been reading *Much Ado About Nothing* and *The Tempest*.

c. John has read *Much Ado About Nothing* and *The Tempest*.

d. The constables have been interrogating Borachio for an hour.

e. Balthazar has been singing Don Pedro's favourite song.

f. Benedick has been in Messina for a week already.

g. Beatrice and Benedick have been arguing again.

h. I have been sitting by Hero's tomb since last night.

i. The cook has been baking cakes.

j. The cook has baked some cakes.

Page 91 – exercise 3

Possible answer

Dear Ferdinand,

Here in Messina there has been much ado about nothing! Everybody is going crazy, including me! Do you remember how I used to say that I would never surrender to one woman. Well now I am different. I am in love, really! And I am in love with a woman I used to hate. Her name is Beatrice and we always used to make fun of each other. But all that has changed. My best friend Claudio has changed too, twice! Like me he used to say that he would never fall in love, and then he fell in love with the Governor of Messina's daughter, Hero. After that, all he thought about was her, and he no longer talked about the army or other interesting things. Just Hero. Now he thinks that Hero has betrayed him and he never wants to see her again; and Beatrice wants me to fight Claudio because of his rudeness to Hero! What a mess!

Please send me some advice.

Your loyal friend,

Benedick

Women in Shakespeare's Comedies

Page 93 – exercise 1

a. Because they were considered by the city authorities to be immoral institutions.

b. Men or boys.

c. He wrote several plays in which women disguised themselves as men.

d. He created strong, independent and intelligent female characters.

e. By love or marriage.

f. They fight a war of wits.

g. Their mutual attraction.

Page 94 – exercise 1

a. Claudio does not wish to fight Leonato because Leonato is an old man.

b. Although he believes that Hero is dead, the Prince is still convinced that she was guilty.

c. At first, Claudio is happy to see Benedick because he hopes that Benedick will cheer him up.

d. Benedick comes to ask Claudio to fight but the Prince thinks that Benedick came to joke with his friend.

e. Benedick will tell everyone that he is a coward if Claudio refuses to fight him.

f. Dogberry has discovered that Borachio and Conrad have told lies about a lady of Messina.

g. Borachio tells Don Pedro that Don John planned to deceive him and Claudio.

Chapter Nine

Page 103 – exercise 1

a. T

b. F – Now, after what the Friar said, he is convinced of her innocence.

c. F – He does not want to serve him because he thinks that he is responsible in part for Hero's death.

d. T

e. F – She does not realise that she is part of the plan.

f. T

g. T

h. F – He has great difficulty writing his very simple poem.

Page 104 – exercise 2

a. Don Pedro and Claudio made Benedick think that Beatrice was in love with him.

b. Before Benedick met Beatrice, he had not let any woman love him.

c. Don John's hatred of his brother does not let him live in peace.

d. Leonato is going to let Claudio marry Hero.

e. As we can see in this play love makes people do strange things.

f. Antonio is not going to let his brother fight Claudio.

g. Dogberry lets drunks go home.

h. Leonato did not let Don John escape.

i. Leonato has not let Claudio know that Hero is really alive.

Page 105 – exercise 3

Possible answer

Dear Harriet,

I know you think that Shakespeare is boring. But I've got the film of *Much Ado About Nothing* because I am sure you'll love it. First of all, it's filled with great actors that you have already seen. There's Keanu Reeves, who was fantastic in *Speed*. Michael Keaton has a comic role in this film. Do you remember how funny he was in *Beetle Juice*?

Maybe you don't know the director of this film, Kenneth Branagh, but he and the actress Emma Thompson have lovers' quarrels in this film and they are quite realistic since the two were actually married at the time!

Also, I have read a number of reviews of this film, all of them favourable. A certain James Berardinelli said that 'Those who don't find Shakespeare's comedies funny, this is the film to see, because it's hilarious.'

Anyway, all of Branagh's earlier films based on Shakespeare have been hits with the general public, and, anyway, it was filmed in the beautiful Tuscan countryside, so if you do find it boring in the end, you can always enjoy the lovely scenery.

Think about it!

Page 106 – exercise 1

a. F – Claudio composed it.

b. T

c. F – He believes that it was all Don John's fault.

d. F – He believes that he is going to marry Antonio's daughter. He is, instead, going to marry Hero.

e. F – He still wants to marry Beatrice.

f. T

Chapter Ten

Page 113 – exercise 1

1. c. / **2. d.** / **3. a.** / **4. c.** / **5. c.**

Page 114 – exercise 2

1b. **1** seriously / **2** earned / **3** lady-in-waiting
1 constables / **2** interrogate / **3** wedding

2d. **1** rotten gift / **2** plot / **3** wickedness / **4** tremble
1 dishonour / **2** guilty / **3** pretend / **4** funeral

3a. **1** each other / **2** enemy / **3** friend
1 innocent / **2** mistake / **3** epitaph / **4** cousin

4c. **1** tomb / **2** mask / **3** gasped / **4** tears
1 poem / **2** letter / **3** although / **4** hands

A lot of bother about love

Page 116 – exercise 1

Possible answer

'Much ado about nothing' is used in modern English to mean that someone or some people create a whole mess about nothing in particular. It is similar in meaning to 'a storm in a tea cup'. Shakespeare might have given this play this title for two reasons. First, he might really be in agreement with Beatrice and Benedick at the beginning of the play and think that love is just nonsense. His play shows what a fragile and changeable emotion love is, and all the ridiculous things that people do for it. After all, the lines he gives to Beatrice and Benedick at the beginning of the play are really good and convincing!

On the other hand, the 'nothing' of the title might refer to all the doubts and problems created when lovers don't trust the one they love or when they don't have the courage to face their real emotions. Beatrice and Benedick fight and argue, and for what? Nothing! In the end they finally admit they love each other.

Then there is Claudio who allows himself to be tricked by Don John, even though he probably knew that Don John was not such a good fellow. So in the story there is a funeral with the right woman and wedding with the wrong woman. And for what? Nothing!

Page 116 – exercise 2

Open answer.

Lines from Shakespeare

Page 116 – exercise 1

a. This is the beginning of the play, and Beatrice is asking the messenger about Benedick's new friend.

b. Benedick is explaining how he will never fall in love.

c. Beatrice, in her witty fashion, is explaining why she will never marry.

d. This is the scene where they trick Benedick into believing that Beatrice loves him.

e. Benedick is beginning to believe that Beatrice loves him.

f. Dogberry is giving orders to his men for their guard duty that night.

g. This is the wedding scene when Claudio speaks badly of Hero because he thinks that she has betrayed him.

h. This is the final exchange of insults between Benedick and Beatrice before they marry.

Page 116 – exercise 2

a. Why then take no note of him, but let him go, and presently call the rest of the watch together, and thank God you are rid of a knave.
(f – Act Three Scene 3)

b. Come, I will have thee, but by this light, I take thee for pity.
(h – Act Five Scene 4)

c. O, when she had writ it and was reading it over, she found Benedick and Beatrice between the sheet?
(d – Act Two Scene 3)

d. I would not deny you, but by this good day, I yield upon great persuasion, and partly to save your life, for I was told you were in a consumption.
(h – Act Five Scene 4)

e. Well, if ever thou dost fall from this faith, thou wilt prove a notable argument.
(b – Act One Scene 1)

f. She's but the sign and semblance of her honour.
(g – Act Four Scene1)

KEY TO THE EXIT TEST

Focus on the context

a. In Stratford-upon-Avon in 1564.
b. Latin.
c. Thirty eight.
d. Between 1598 and 1599.
e. It's a comedy about love.

Focus on the story

1. C 2. B 3. D 4. A 5. B 6. D
7. C 8. C 9. D 10. A 11. C
12. D

3

a. False – Leonato, the Governor of Messina, had one daughter, Hero and one niece, Beatrice.
b. False – She was always very rude about him.
c. True
d. True
e. True
f. False – She always did what her father told her to. She was a very dutiful daughter.
g. False – She spoke to Benedick.
h. True
i. False – The intention was for Beatrice to overhear them talking.
j. False – He said he looked sad because he had a toothache.
k. True
l. False – She fainted on the day of her wedding to Claudio and then everyone pretended she really had died.
m. True
n. True
o. False – He agreed to marry Hero's cousin.
p. True

146

Black Cat English Readers

BLACK CAT ENGLISH CLUB
Membership Application Form

BLACK CAT ENGLISH CLUB is for those who love English reading and seek for better English to share and learn with fun together.

Benefits offered:
- *Membership Card*
- *Member badge, poster, bookmark*
- *Book discount coupon*
- *Black Cat English Reward Scheme*
- *English learning e-forum*
- *Surprise gift and more...*

Simply fill out the application form below and fax it back to 2565 1113.

Join Now! It's FREE exclusively for readers who have purchased *Black Cat English Readers* !

The book(or book set) that you have purchased: _____

English Name: _____ (Surname) _____ (Given Name)

Chinese Name: _____

Address: _____

Tel: _____ Fax: _____

Email: _____

Sex: ❏ Male   ❏ Female   (Login password for e-forum will be sent to this email address.)

Education Background: ❏ Primary 1-3   ❏ Primary 4-6   ❏ Junior Secondary Education (F1-3)
                     ❏ Senior Secondary Education (F4-5)   ❏ Matriculation
                     ❏ College   ❏ University or above

Age: ❏ 6 - 9   ❏ 10 - 12   ❏ 13 - 15   ❏ 16 - 18   ❏ 19 - 24   ❏ 25 - 34
     ❏ 35 - 44   ❏ 45 - 54   ❏ 55 or above

Occupation: ❏ Student   ❏ Teacher   ❏ White Collar   ❏ Blue Collar
             ❏ Professional ❏ Manager   ❏ Business Owner   ❏ Housewife
             ❏ Others (please specify: _____)

As a member, what would you like **BLACK CAT ENGLISH CLUB** to offer:
   ❏ Member gathering/ party   ❏ English class with native teacher   ❏ English competition
   ❏ Newsletter   ❏ Online sharing   ❏ Book fair
   ❏ Book discount   ❏ Others (please specify: _____)

Other suggestions to **BLACK CAT ENGLISH CLUB:**

_____

Please sign here: _____

(Date: _____)